SECRETS IN THE SAND

When Sarah Daniels moves to a sleepy Cornish village her neighbour, local handyman and champion surfer, Ben Trelawny is intrigued. He falls in love with her stunning looks and quirky ways — but who is this woman? Why does she lock herself in her cottage — and why is she so guarded? When Ben finally gets past Sarah's barriers, a national newspaper reporter arrives in the village. Sarah disappears, making a decision that puts her life and future in jeopardy.

JANE RETALLICK

SECRETS IN THE SAND

Complete and Unabridged

LINFORD
Leicester

First published in Great Britain in 2011

First Linford Edition
published 2012

British Library CIP Data

Retallick, Jane.
Secrets in the sand. - -
(Linford romance library)
1. Love stories.
2. Large type books.
I. Title II. Series
823.9′2–dc23

ISBN 978–1–4448–1073–8

Published by
F. A. Thorpe (Publishing)
Anstey, Leicestershire

Set by Words & Graphics Ltd.
Anstey, Leicestershire
Printed and bound in Great Britain by
T. J. International Ltd., Padstow, Cornwall

This book is printed on acid-free paper

1

Sarah sighed with relief as she dropped the last packing crate on to the floor of her new house. It wasn't the departure that she'd imagined — a successful daughter, wife and mother making her way in life. Instead, she was just a lone figure driving off into a harsh and unforgiving world, right into a thunderstorm judging by the menacing clouds gathering overhead and the humidity that suffocated her every pore.

She'd made her excuses to leave earlier than planned — traffic, weather, needing to arrive before dark — she'd used them all. It was unbearable to be there any more. She had to get away — two hundred and fifty-eight miles away, to be exact, to a remote Cornish village. That should be far enough.

The evening sun poured into the living room, massaging its warmth into her sore muscles. The house was bare and the paint tatty from years of being battered and bruised, but Sarah's heart lifted at the thought of transforming it into her sanctuary.

Here there were no hidden corners, no memories, no nightmares. She could start afresh, write her own history from now on and be in control of her life. Nobody would ever take that away from her again.

She searched through the keys in the estate agent's envelope and found the one that she was looking for. The patio door was stiff, but a good tug released it from its shackles and sweet, fresh air filled Sarah's lungs. She stepped out and drank in the stunning view.

Golden sand stretched for miles ahead of her, accessed by a battered wooden gate at the bottom of her overgrown garden. The waves rode strongly up the beach on the incoming tide and seagulls soared overhead. It was like leaving hell and arriving in heaven, she thought.

Sarah listened. She inhaled the silence, the peace, the freedom. It was a stark contrast to the last two years of chaos, the sterile stench of hospitals, the funeral, people everywhere intruding into all the private details of her life, the court room and the unspeakable horrors that followed.

Now she could clean them out of her system, move on, be free and single. No hassles, no more being hunted. It was the life she'd craved and visualised for so long. The fantasies that got her through the darkest days.

Stepping back into the house, she carefully locked the patio door, then deadlocked the front and back doors. Tomorrow she'd look in the phone book and find someone who could change the locks for her. She needed to make sure that she was the only one with keys.

Sarah hung her portable door alarms on the handles and breathed a sigh of relief. It would be okay now; a new start in a new place where nobody knew her.

She could get on with her life, absorb herself in her hobbies and art and forget the past. It was over; finally, it was all over.

She sank to the floor and sobbed.

★ ★ ★

'Hey, Ben, whatever happened to you?' a friendly voice exclaimed.

Ben glanced up and saw his work-mate Darren silhouetted harshly against the bright sunlight.

'Oh, man, don't ask,' he replied, shaking his head in dismay.

His surfboard lay carefully balanced on two battered chairs in the middle of a very messy garage. Ben studied it with a critical eye. It was devastating that the rough surf yesterday had snapped his fin. But, if he was honest with himself, he'd known the dangers when he'd chosen to go out in it.

The thrill of mastering the biggest waves that the local surfers had seen all season had been simply irresistible, and turning down a challenge was just not in his nature. He held most of the local and county trophies and had been surfing since he was knee-high to a grasshopper, as his grandad had always said proudly.

'I misjudged the surfing conditions,' Ben explained. 'It's been a long afternoon! Fancy a coffee?'

He walked over and flicked the switch on the kettle that was hiding amongst some paint tins and random pots of nails and screws.

'It'll have to be black — milk goes off too quickly in this heat and I can't be bothered to go indoors to get some.'

Darren gave a slow, long whistle. Ben turned to see what had caught his attention. Passing the house was a little silver Vauxhall Corsa which then turned off down the long driveway opposite.

'I think your new neighbours have arrived at last,' he said. 'Well, well.'

Ben straightened up and watched the car disappear behind some trees. It had taken a long time to find a buyer for the old place and the whole event was shrouded in mystery.

He watched for a minute, then sloshed boiling water into a chipped, stained mug, added some instant coffee granules and gave it a good stir with an old screwdriver.

'I wonder who they are?' Darren said, putting up his hand to refuse the offer of a drink. 'I love a good story for the darts night at the pub!'

Nobody had seen or spoken to the owner, and rumour had it that an intermediary had been used.

A twinge of sadness nipped at Ben.

'It'll always be Elsie's house to me,' he said firmly, directing his eyes back to the surfboard. Elsie had been like a grandmother to him and her death a year ago still held some rawness.

'Aren't you just a little bit curious?' Darren asked. 'I mean, the rumours flying around the village have been pretty hot! Anyway, I'd better shoot off. Things to do, people to see, you know.' He flashed a big grin at Ben and headed off towards the beach.

Ben sighed. He really wasn't that interested; he'd heard everything.

There were assumptions that the new owner, or owners, might have moved back from abroad or were using the house as a second home. Then there were the more scandalous fancies — a rich man buying it for his mistress, or drug dealers hoping for an inconspicuous place to grow their cannabis. It had even been suggested that spiritual leaders wanted to use it to channel messages from the other side.

Ben had soon got bored of listening to the village gossips.

Judging by the sight of the battered car half-filled with belongings, this was a pretty ordinary house move. He'd only got a quick glimpse of a young woman on her own, but perhaps her husband was coming along later with a second car full of stuff.

Certainly there hadn't been much stuff in the first one — he'd taken more with him when he'd gone to college.

He flung back the last of his coffee and made another close examination of his surfboard. He had more important things to be doing than sticking his nose into business that had nothing to do with him.

★ ★ ★

Amy stood at the sink peeling potatoes. Ben loved living with his younger sister and two-year-old niece, Tegan. They were caring and fun — and Amy was an amazing cook. She had been a great support to him when Paula had left him after a long and turbulent eight-year relationship.

His heart ached for a moment at that thought, and he shook his head to rid himself of the memories and bring him back to the incredible smell coming from the oven.

'Did you see our new neighbours arrive? Isn't it exciting?' Amy carefully took aim and lobbed another potato at the pot.

'Well, I'm not really that bothered.' Ben peeked through the oven door. 'And I've only seen one neighbour so far. There was a woman driving the silver car and no more have gone past since.' Ben wiped his dirty, waxy hands on a tea towel.

'Ben! How many times . . . ?'

He grimaced, threw the towel into the washing machine and made his way to the sink for a proper wash.

'Anyway, I was thinking,' Amy neatly swung the pan of potatoes on to the cooker whilst simultaneously removing a pan of carrots. Ben marvelled at her ability to multi-task. 'I was thinking that it would be nice if one of us went over later, once they've had some time to settle in, and give them that saffron cake that's almost ready.'

'My favourite cake!' Ben protested, shaking his hands dry and perching on the kitchen stool. He didn't think that new neighbours were *that* special.

'Well, they're foreigners, you know. Well — foreign to these parts, anyhow.

Might make them feel a bit more welcome. You can't start being Cornish until you've tasted a saffron cake.'

'Once they've tasted your saffron cake, they'll never want to leave!'

'Just like you then,' his sister rebuked. She affectionately tousled his hair. 'Really, Ben, your hair's stiff with salt. Don't you ever use conditioner after you've been for a surf?'

Ben wondered sometimes whether his sister and mother had swapped bodies when he hadn't been looking. But at the moment he was more concerned about the loss of his beloved treat.

'Well, can't you take them some pasties instead?' he pleaded. 'I mean, they're just as much part of Cornish tradition as saffron cake. Then we can tell them all about the miners and the pixies, proper Cornish folklore.'

Amy rolled her eyes. 'Really Benjamin, I think Tegan is better at sharing than you! For your sins, I'm now allocating the job to you. And you'd better not ask if you can join them for tea and cake on the pretence of showing them how to eat it, or I'll skin your hide.'

Ben wished he had a good excuse for not going over the road later, but he had no other plans and Amy knew it. Well, he would do his duty, say a quick hello and then leave them — or her — to get on with unpacking.

A groan escaped his lips and earned him a teasing whack around the head with a clean tea towel.

* * *

It was nearly eight o'clock by the time Sarah had pumped up her airbed, unpacked some of her food and bedding and checked that her phone and broadband connection was up and running as promised. She'd do a massive online shop tomorrow and sort out her home comforts.

This was going to be the home she'd never had, and sleeping on the floor was not part of the plan of how her new future would be. It was still quite light outside, so she enjoyed pottering around the house while showing no external signs of life.

She paused for a moment and visualised herself as invisible, as if no living soul knew that she existed on this earth any more. She stretched out her arms and luxuriated in the feeling. This was how she wanted it to be, forever if possible. Just her and her own life.

Sarah pulled the last pair of curtains out of her bin bag and dragged them up the stairs. She thought they'd just about fit her bedroom window. She was very grateful that a curtain pole, despite being a little wonky, still seemed to be securely attached to the wall.

Climbing on to an old wooden crate that she'd found in the cellar, she reached up to start looping the curtain hooks on to their fittings. As each one clicked neatly into place, Sarah felt a sense of calm wash over her.

From her elevated position, she could see out over the small village, little houses just starting to twinkle like fairy lights across the landscape as dusk fell. It was so pretty and peaceful, she thought.

'Come on little curtain,' she said out loud. 'Just one more hook and then we're done. Welcome to our new home. We're going to be very happy here, aren't we?' The last curtain ring slid into position and she ran her hands down the length of the fabric so it hung freely. Then, pausing for a moment, she fingered the light green velour, enjoying its softness and warmth.

She lifted her eyes and gazed at the chaos that was her new front garden. It was like an ugly lump of clay waiting to be kneaded, smoothed and shaped into a beautiful piece of art.

She could just imagine it now, filled with beautiful, colourful flowers, roses over the arch by the gate and perennial shrubs in the darker corners to give a sense of completeness to the garden.

Her thoughts were abruptly interrupted by a glimpse of a figure behind her hedge by the front gate. Automatically, she drew the curtain around her like a cocoon then slowly eased a sliver back to create a small hole between the curtain and window frame.

Taking care not to move more than necessary, she peeped through it, one eye squinting acutely to make out the details. Who was it and what were they doing?

She could feel the heat starting to course through her veins. As her heart thumped loudly, she stayed on red alert, frozen and stiff. She prayed that nobody had seen her.

After all, she was supposed to be safe here, wasn't she? That's what people had said. What if they were wrong and it was all about to start again?

She watched like a rabbit hiding from a fox. Oh no, he was opening the front gate. From a distance, she couldn't see him that well. He looked a bit hesitant, though. Acting suspiciously, she thought, his eyes devouring the house, his gait slow. And what was in that bag?

Alarm bells rang. Sarah slowly inched

her way down inside the curtain and gently rolled off the crate on to the floor. Stooping to stay out of view of the window, she made her way to the door then on to the landing.

Silently, she moved to sit on the top stair, her hands trembling. She could hear her heart thudding loudly in her head. From this position, she calculated that she could use either the back or front doors or the kitchen window as escape routes if necessary.

She waited with dread, too scared to think about what might happen next. Sarah's fingers gripped the edge of the stair as if she was going to be wrenched from her hiding place and burnt at the stake.

Then it came, a bullet-like rap, tap, tap on the door. She huddled out of sight of the letterbox and desperately wished that he would go away. After what seemed like an eternity, the knock came again, louder this time. She held her breath as if the slightest movement could betray her.

A trickle of sweat ran coldly down Sarah's back and panic pulsed in waves over her.

The man tried the door handle, and one hundred decibels of high pitched wailing shrieked through the darkness. She heard his quick footsteps retreat down the path.

What on earth was she doing here?

2

The June morning dawned bright and with a light breeze. The surfing conditions were perfect and Ben was determined to make the most of his early-morning surf before work. He stuffed another generous slice of saffron cake into his mouth and pushed the carrier bag back into his tool cupboard.

There was no need to tell Amy about his superbly failed attempt to make himself known to his neighbours. Not quite yet, anyway. He still had three quarters of the cake to polish off.

He shrugged his shoulders and decided that a surfing session would clear away the uneasy feelings left over from last night.

Well, at least he'd got the saffron cake out of it. He was sure he could manage to eat most of it before he had to confess that it had never quite reached its destination. He felt he deserved it after going through all that.

Ben eased himself into his wetsuit and grabbed his board. Living two hundred feet from the beach was just incredible, a surfer's dream.

He'd had enough of women. All he needed was the exhilaration of riding the waves, mastering their twists and turns, and being carried away by their sheer exhilarating power.

Closing the garage door, Ben gave a little cheer and headed towards the surf. As he crossed the beach, he could feel the spray on his skin and taste the salt on his lips. This was ultimate contentment, he thought, as his legs collided with the first waves. Just him and the sea.

Diving under the surface, he shivered briefly as the cold water flooded into the gap between his wetsuit and his skin before heating up to body temperature. The Atlantic rollers beckoned him as he jumped flat on to his board and started paddling out to where the larger waves were starting to build up to a massive crescendo.

Watching and waiting, he moved in for his first ride of the day.

As he drove his board on with the first wave, dipping and plunging as it broke strongly on its journey to the shore, Ben forgot about the events of the night before. Life was good.

★ ★ ★

Sarah hadn't got to sleep until the early hours of the morning but the summer sun, which flooded through every little gap in her newly-hung curtains, nudged her awake.

For a moment she didn't know where she was.

'Dad?' she called out in a sleepy limbo. She rolled over. The bed had leaked some air overnight. Sinking under her weight, it released her in a tangled mess of sheets on to the floor. Shaken out of her reverie, Sarah opened her eyes properly and looked around the bare room with a start. Suddenly, life before the move seemed a whole world away.

'I'm in my new house in Cornwall. Today is the first day of my new life,' she resolutely told herself. 'The past is in the past. Forget about it.'

The memory of the intruder flashed back into her head and unsettled her. She jumped up, wrapped her dressing gown around her and ran downstairs with trepidation.

Everything was exactly as she'd left it and her body relaxed as she switched off her door alarms. The sound of the morning songbirds caught her attention.

Moving the edge of the curtain ajar, she peered outside. It was a beautiful morning, so fresh and clean. Her heart leapt in excitement as she wondered what treasures the tide had left on the sand.

She was itching to get back to her art, reignite some passion in her soul. The brightness of the sunshine wiped out the fears of last night, its cheerful beams promising optimism and hope.

It was still only six o'clock. Sarah felt confident that the beach would be her own at this time of the day. It would be at least another hour before the dog walkers and early morning joggers emerged, she guessed.

She had a quick wash in refreshingly cold water, making a mental note to herself to find out how to turn the boiler on later, and threw on her comfy jeans and T-shirt.

At the end of the garden path, Sarah gave the bolt on the rickety wooden gate a sharp tug. When it shot free, she found herself supporting the gate as it balanced on one hinge. She added another item to her mental to-do list. Being busy was good, she told herself — less time for her to sit and dwell on everything else.

The beach stretched like freshly spun gold for miles in front of her, the sunlight dancing off the water. The breeze tempted her towards the shore-line as gulls cried above her. Sarah drank in the beauty and wildness of the view and felt all her stress evaporate.

She kicked off her flip flops, leaving them behind her hedge, and whooped in sheer joy, racing along the sand with her arms spread wide and her face held up to the clear blue sky. The ocean spray kissed her cheeks and the damp grittiness of the sand moulded to her feet, massaging between her toes.

Feeling like a carefree child, Sarah sprinted along the beach before collaps-ing breathless and ecstatic on to a rock. She had forgotten how amazing it felt to be at one with nature, outside in harmony with the world. She wanted to do so much — dip her toes in the icy sea water, comb the shoreline to see what the tide had left behind, create sand art and explore the rock pools.

And the best thing of all was that she could. She could do anything she wanted. For the first time in many months, nobody was stopping her. She was her own woman again.

* * *

Ben rubbed the moisture from his eyes and spluttered the thick water out of his lungs. He cursed loudly.

He'd been riding the most incredible wave and then found himself abruptly deposited back in the sea during a really exciting moment. He'd been balancing beautifully on top of a massive breaker then the board had slipped from under his feet and he'd gone with it.

'Dude, did you just bail on that wave?' Kai, a fellow surfer, cracked a joke in his strong Australian accent. He paddled closer to Ben. 'I never had you down as a quitter!'

Still coughing, Ben kicked hard to keep his head above the water as another wave swept past him.

'Wretched thing,' he said, determined to discover what had gone so wrong. Pulling on his rope, he brought his board back to him and clung on to it to keep himself afloat whilst he examined it.

'It's the fin, again. It's still isn't right, darn it.'

Kai looked at him with sympathy. 'I think it's about time you took it down to the surf shop.'

Ben reluctantly agreed. It was a massive inconvenience, not to mention the cost. Surely his week could only get better from now on?

He spat out some more sea water.

'Looks like I'm done for today. Sorry, mate,' he said and started awkwardly padding back inland.

As he dragged his board on to the sand, he noticed a lone figure enjoying the solitude of the beach. She looked vaguely familiar, but from a distance he couldn't make out any details. He wanted to get home and climb into a hot shower but there was something about her that caught his eye. He stood for ages, admiring her graceful movements across the sand.

Sometimes she gave a little skip and jump, reminding him of a prize filly; lithe, elegant and spirited. He watched as she walked away from the tide line, arms full of odds and ends that had been carried in by the sea overnight. Usually the spoils consisted of a variety of battered and empty plastic containers, old bits of rope, fishing gear and other tat.

Beachcomber, he thought. *She must be a holidaymaker.* At that moment, she turned and headed towards the sea, stopping halfway to pick up a stick. He watched as she wrote something in the sand, walked a bit further, then wrote something else.

Ben wasn't surprised. The whole beach was covered with heart shapes filled with initials like 'R luvs T'. The sand was an irresistible blank canvas to everyone who visited. It was like a magic blackboard, scribbled on and then carefully erased by each high tide, ready for the next love-struck scribes to decorate anew.

The woman walked up to the ocean and let the first wave trickle over her toes. She hesitated as her feet adjusted to the coldness of the water, then walked in a little deeper, up to ankle depth, and started to stride along the shore in his direction.

As the surf splashed her rolled up jeans, she didn't seem to mind that she was getting wet. Her white T-shirt clung to her body in the breeze, emphasising the roundness of her breasts and her narrow waist. She was clearly oblivious to his presence.

He suddenly felt self-conscious, like someone who was spying on a scene that was intensely private. He walked a little further up the beach but, despite his good intentions to go home, he just couldn't resist gazing back at the stranger.

As she got closer, he noticed the faraway expression on her face — as if she was in another world. She didn't even notice when some of her newly acquired treasures slipped out of her arms into the wet sand.

Ben felt torn. For some reason it didn't feel right to rush after her and give her the things she'd dropped. He'd feel as if he was intruding on a precious moment, perhaps one that would never be recaptured.

But as he watched the waves creep towards the gnarled wood and small plastic bag, he couldn't stop himself being the good Samaritan and rescuing them from the incoming tide. Clutching his board, he hurried back to the water and grabbed them as they threatened to float away back to where they had come from.

The woman was now about two hundred metres up ahead of him. He hesitated briefly, still unsure about his choice of action, but then marched resolutely after her.

'Excuse me!' he called loudly but she didn't appear to hear him, his words whipped behind him in the wind. She was walking quite briskly and he had to rush to catch up with her.

The surfboard felt heavy and cumbersome when he had his other hand full with stuff. His arms ached. He hoped his efforts were worth it for a bit of wood and a bag of something that he hadn't looked at, but had clearly been collected for a reason. Finally he got close enough.

'Excuse me! You've dropped something,' he shouted. The woman spun around as if he'd fired a shot. He was stunned for a moment. Looking back at him were the most incredible bright blue eyes set in a small face with a cute button nose, framed by dark curls. He almost forgot for a moment why he had stopped her in the first place.

'I'm sorry?' she asked in a cool tone.

The illusion shattered. Ben found his tongue and held out his left hand.

'I noticed you drop these. I thought you wouldn't want to lose them so I picked them up.' He hesitated then, getting no reply, said, 'It's so breezy that it was hard to make you hear me but I thought you'd want them back. So, er . . . here they are.'

He was rambling and standing there with an outstretched arm full of junk like an idiot. What was wrong with him?

'Thank you.' Her tone was civil but uninviting. She took her things from him and her body turned in preparation to end the conversation. Despite all the negative signals, Ben felt compelled to keep talking.

'It's a lovely morning for a walk along the beach, isn't it?' His insides quivered and he attempted to mask his uncharacteristic nervousness by putting a broad smile on his face. 'It's such a beautiful area,' he went on. 'Have you been here before?'

There was a moment's silence, during which he sensed that his presence was very unwelcome.

'Thank you for returning my things.' The woman gave him a cursory glance, then turned and walked off.

Ben felt peeved and intrigued at the same time. It was unusual for someone round here not to exchange pleasantries. Holidaymakers were usually keen to talk to the locals and discuss the weather, the best surfing spots and good eating places. The aloofness of this woman was unusual, to say the least.

He turned and walked back along the shore but he couldn't rid himself of thoughts of the encounter. The woman's beauty alone was unforgettable, even though she had shunned his efforts to be friendly. He couldn't remember the last time he had let a woman affect him like that. After Paula, he had vowed to enjoy being single and not let women spoil his life.

As Ben walked up the beach, a seagull landed near him with a beak filled with chips. One day, he mused, gulls might actually stop eating junk food and start catching fish again. The bird managed to rearrange its ambitious mouthful and took off. It was then that Ben noticed some markings on the sand next to where it had stood.

His curiosity piqued, he strolled closer and read the writing.

'I AM SARAH DANIELS FOREVER' it said. So, that was what that woman was called! It seemed a strange thing to write, though. He turned to go home then remembered that he had seen her write something else, too.

Making his way back further down the beach, Ben found it next to the stick that she'd discarded. The waves were getting closer, poised to do their daily cleaning duties.

'I AM FREE, FREE, FREE!' it read.

Ben's face lit up — that meant she must be single! A smile fleetingly swept over his face before the old, unpleasant memories flooded back into his head. He picked up the stick and wrote his own message right next to it.

'BEN TRELAWNY. FREE, SINGLE AND HAPPY. WOMEN ARE BANNED.'

He admired his artwork and headed home to get ready for a day's work. Life was much better when it was uncomplicated by relationships. He just had to keep reminding himself of that.

3

Sarah scrubbed furiously at the dirt ingrained on the old white hob. So far that morning, she'd done some online shopping, cleaned the bedrooms, bathroom and stairs, removing copious amounts of dust from every nook and cranny. The house had been empty for a while and she suspected that its previous occupant had started neglecting it long before it had been put on to the market.

Now she was tackling the kitchen, which was proving to be grimy enough to be ideal for venting her emotions.. She had been trying to forget about that surfer who'd rudely interrupted the perfect end to her perfect walk. He'd had some cheek, trying to turn on his charm and draw her into conversation.

Typical surfer, she thought; *trying to chat up every woman who walked by.*

As if the sight of a toned male in a black skin-tight wetsuit was going to have her falling at his feet. Those days were well and truly over for her.

She tackled the last of the dirt with extra vigour in an attempt to get rid of more unwelcome thoughts. The image was etched on her brain and refused to budge, even more stubborn than the dirt she was cleaning.

Ben had been standing there in the brilliant sunshine with fresh water droplets glistening on his raven-black hair and when he had smiled, two dimples in his cheeks lit up his face. The wetsuit hadn't left much to the imagination and she could see that he clearly took care of his body.

She had tried not to pay much attention to him, though she hadn't meant to be as rude as she felt she'd come across. After all, it was very kind of him to come after her and perhaps he was just trying to be friendly. Cornish people were kind folk; that's one reason that she'd chosen to come here, away from the hostile city environment.

Pushing away her guilt at her earlier behaviour, she wiped the hob dry, peeled off her rubber gloves and dialled a number on the phone. It was answered on almost the second ring.

'Good morning, Tremaine's Handyman Service, Joe speaking. How can I help?' The voice on the other end had a strong and gentle Cornish burr. A vision of an ageing local man, his face weathered by the elements, working long past retirement came into her head. She smiled to herself. It was a good feeling. She wondered when she had last allowed herself such a luxury. Sometimes she felt three hundred years old rather than thirty.

'I was wondering if someone could come round, preferably today, and change the locks on my back and front doors. I've already got the replacements, they just need fitting. I've moved into Shell Cottage.'

'Oh, old Elsie's place!' The man's

voice took on a nostalgic tone as he took his time to get to the point. 'Well, it's about time it had some new blood in it. Lock replacements, you said? Not a problem. It's a generous time slot so if there's anything else needing doing, just say. How about two o'clock?'

Sarah agreed and happily ticked another item off her list. Having worked hard for the whole of the morning, she decided that it was time to play. Putting the events of the last twenty-four hours out of her head, she started sifting through her beachcombing spoils.

The living room table wasn't the best place to start her art studio but it would do until she got herself sorted out. Covering its worn, varnished surface with a white sheet, she started arranging bits of driftwood, rope and shells until the scene satisfied her. Rummaging through her art bag for her drawing pad and pencils, she was itching to get started.

The warmth of the sunshine flooded into the room and she opened the patio door to welcome in the coolness of the breeze and sound of the birds and sea, then she sat, surrounded by her materials, and time slipped away as she soon became absorbed herself in her sketching.

$$\star \quad \star \quad \star$$

Ben kicked open the front door, one arm full of dust sheets, the other holding a massive toolbox. The start of his working week hadn't been too bad. One shoebox-sized bathroom to paint and a few roof tiles to hammer back into position were jobs that were well within his capacity.

The memories of his early-morning encounter were distant, pushed aside by the concentration needed to work and chatter to his customers at the same time. He loved his job, but providing company to elderly people whilst trying to do his work to his usual high standard was a challenge.

His stomach rumbled and he dropped

everything in a neat pile on the polished hall floor, slamming the door behind him.

'Is that you, Ben?' A voice came down from upstairs. He groaned inwardly at having his peace shattered already.

'Yes, just come for a quick bite then off again. What are you doing home?' he bellowed back. His head was already in the fridge sniffing out the ham and tomatoes.

'I had a gap between my appointments so I thought I'd give myself an extended lunch break,' Amy shouted.

His sister was a mobile hairdresser which fitted perfectly around being a single mother and childcare arrangements. Living with a hairdresser did mean that it was sometimes a struggle to get into the bathroom, though. He couldn't understand how women needed to take so long just to fiddle with a bit of make-up and hair. He was a splash-and-dash man himself. It made life a lot simpler.

Ben cut himself two thick slices of bread, covered them with butter and filled them with a generous helping of ham topped with home-grown tomatoes. *This is the best thing about being single,* he thought, *being able to eat anything without having a stick-thin girlfriend glaring jealously at you across the table while tucking into her crispbread and cottage cheese.*

He took a big bite and savoured the combination of the flavours. Today wasn't turning out too badly after all, he thought.

Amy made her way carefully down the stairs. He did a double take. Her hair was drawn tightly back, her face was covered in a frog-slime grey face mask and she walked like someone with severe rickets.

'Just waiting for my toe nail polish to dry,' she said in way of explanation after clocking his bafflement. 'But before I forget — '

Ben wondered what else was going to be added to his list of jobs today. Or perhaps she was going to ask about his visit to the neighbours last night? He felt that the first one was much more desirable. He wasn't quite ready to reveal the fate of the saffron cake quite yet. He held his breath and attempted to look casual.

'Is there something you'd like done?' he asked in an attempt to steer the conversation in a good direction.

'No, it's just your mobile wasn't working earlier so Old Joe rang the house. Mrs Parsons has cancelled her grass-cutting this afternoon, and so has Mr Royland after her, but another job's come in instead. That new neighbour wants her locks changed, so the job's yours. Darren's too busy.'

Ben sat in an awkward silence, wishing he could delegate this particular job to someone else.

Amy continued, 'Joe said he forgot to ask her name but I said it would be okay as you only met her yesterday. Oh, and apparently you can finish a bit early considering you worked overtime last week so I called the childminder and told her that you'd be collecting Tegan today.'

A heavy feeling landed in Ben's stomach. Suddenly his sandwich tasted like a soggy cardboard mess. Amy took another look at him.

'Are you okay? That job's not a problem, is it?'

'No, of course not.' Ben decided that he couldn't totally lie to his sister. 'But there was no reply last night when I went over so I didn't actually make it as far as introductions. Anyway, your face mask looks like it's ready to come off. Shall I make you a sandwich for after?' He hastily tried to re-divert the conversation.

'Yes, that would be great. Thanks Ben.' Amy started heading back upstairs, then paused and turned around. 'Hold on a minute. So where's the saffron cake, then?'

★ ★ ★

Sarah sat absorbed in her sketch, her fingers working deftly and quickly. She'd forgotten how satisfying it was to see a picture taking shape. The pencil scratched happily away on the paper as she captured the roughness of the twisted driftwood and the gentle curves of the sea shells. She marvelled at their colours and detail.

Nature is so clever, she thought, putting her pencil down for a minute and running her hand over the smoothness of the inside of a mussel shell. The intricate design was just so incredible, right down to a carefully hinged joint that allowed the mussel to open and close over and over again without falling apart.

The measurements were faultless; the shell curved in, then flattened out for just long enough to make a glue line for the ligaments that held it together, yet it was flexible enough to allow the mussel to stretch open to feed. It was amazing. Lost in thought, Sarah felt a very small part of a very big world.

She was brought back to earth by a polite knocking on her door. Jerking, she dropped her shell and turned sharply. She hesitated, hoping they would go away. But the knock was repeated.

'Hello, it's the handyman from Tremaine's. I've come to change your locks,' a voice called from behind the door.

A hurried look at the wall clock shocked her. Two o'clock already? Where had the last couple of hours gone? Brushing the pencil shavings off her soft blue cotton skirt, she leapt up and rushed to the door.

'I'm sorry,' she started to say as she pulled the door open, then she froze. Smiling back at her was the same dimpled greeting that she'd encountered earlier that morning. Her cheeks flushed and she didn't know what to say next. Would he recognise her? And if he did, would he acknowledge her? She instantly regretted her earlier abruptness.

'Um, thank you for coming. The locks are here. And four bolts too. Top and bottom for each door.' Sarah grabbed them off the shelf just inside the door and handed them to him. She didn't know what to do next.

'That's great. I'm Ben, by the way.' He examined her packets. 'You've got good locks here, too.' They stood looking at each other, the awkwardness pronounced.

'Um . . . it would help if I could just come in and see what needs doing . . . '

Sarah blushed even redder. 'Of course, I'm sorry. Yes, it's this door and the one at the back.' *Obviously,* she told herself.

It had been a long time since she'd dealt with workmen. Should she offer him a cup of tea? She didn't really want him hanging around long, though.

Ben left his toolbox outside and stepped into the cottage. The smell of lavender polish hung in the air and every surface gleamed.

'Gosh, you've been busy,' he said. 'I've never seen it so clean in here!'

'You've been in here before?' Sarah's tone was edgy.

'Well, I've lived in the village for many years and I was very close to Elsie, the woman who used to own this place, but she died last summer. I know this house very well.'

Sarah thought she detected a slight wobble in his voice but it was quickly replaced by his usual strong tones.

'So, anyway, you can leave me to get on with things if you want. I know my way around and you must be busy.' Ben turned and made his way back for his tools. Dressed in Old Joe's summer uniform of a T-shirt and shorts, his strong calf muscles caught Sarah's eye and she couldn't help watching him as he went out the door.

Wasn't that what she wanted — for him to leave her alone? And, he didn't seem to acknowledge that they'd already met. So why did she feel a slight pang of disappointment when he didn't seem to need her any more?

★   ★   ★

Half an hour later, Sarah was fiddling with the boiler and reading a tatty instruction booklet with half the pages missing. She turned on the hot tap for the millionth time. The water was still coming out cold.

Sarah didn't know what else it could be and the boiler was badly positioned in a stupid, narrow and bottomless cupboard. You had to stick your head right into it and use a torch, in the middle of a brilliant summer's day, just to read the display.

She felt her annoyance rising. Downstairs she could hear the repeated opening and closing of a door which increasingly grated on her nerves. How long did it take to screw on a couple of locks, for goodness' sake?

Sarah peered at line three of the instructions, complete with its grimy fingerprint which obscured the most essential wording. She attempted to translate the text and jammed her head back in the cupboard. It was very hot and the sweat from her fingers made her hold on the torch slippery.

She held down button one for ten seconds then pressed button two, as instructed. The boiler beeped and the light went out. That wasn't what was supposed to happen. She stretched further into the cupboard in an attempt to get to the boiler reset button.

At that point, the torch fell from her fingers, knocked itself out on a wooden beam and disappeared down into the blackness. She swore loudly and banged her head as she retreated back into the brightness of the bathroom for some fresh oxygen.

She heard a deep laugh behind her. Ben was standing there, watching her with amusement.

'I suppose you think it's funny,' she snapped without thinking. 'It's not my fault this boiler is in such an awkward place and is refusing to work.'

He laughed again and then grinned that irritatingly attractive smile. 'Perhaps it would help if I had a look at it? There's a certain knack to it.'

She reluctantly stepped aside and let him in. He leant into the cupboard, giving her a rear view of his taut lower body. She forced herself to look the other way. She had been happy with her decision to come here to be alone, and nothing was going to make her doubt that.

It was too complicated, anyway; as if any man would ever touch her now.

A loud rumbling noise filled the bathroom and Ben's muffled voice called to her to try the hot tap. She turned it on. This time, tepid water poured out, replaced within minutes by boiling steam.

'Fantastic. I'm glad the old girl is still working.' He slid like a snake back out of the cupboard. 'You don't need to worry about anything now but if you need a hand with your central heating timer in the winter, just give us a shout. Right, let me show you your new locks. They're working fine, but I had to make a few adjustments to get them to fit properly.' He started to make his way back across the landing.

Sarah felt her heart beating fast. It was just the heat, she told herself, it was getting hotter by the minute and that cupboard had been airless. Her throat was so dry that she desperately needed a drink. But she couldn't get one for herself and not offer one to Ben too; it was rude.

Wrenched in two directions, she thought quickly and followed him. She took a deep breath. 'I'm going to get myself a glass of water,' she said. 'Would you like one?'

* * *

Ben looked around at the nearly bare house with curiosity, cradling the ice cool glass in his hands. He still wasn't sure if Sarah was warming to the idea of him being here or not. It was clear that offering him a drink had been because she needed to quench her own thirst rather than considering his.

He felt that he was receiving vibes

that told him to turn the offer down, but he was too fascinated by this enigmatic female. Also, he enjoyed being back in the cottage's familiar surroundings and there was still so much about this mysterious woman that he wanted to find out.

He decided to stick to business talk to answer his first question, keeping things formal and unthreatening. 'I'll need to make you out an invoice for the lock work,' he said, 'but I'm afraid Joe forgot to ask you for your name.'

Sarah stood some distance from him, looking into the garden. 'It's Sarah,' she said quietly. 'Sarah Daniels.'

So that was his first hurdle jumped. He hadn't liked to tell her that he already knew, that he'd been snooping at her writing in the sand. Better to get introductions done in a traditional way, really, particularly given that she was not the friendliest woman he'd ever met. Yet those intense blue eyes held a strange spell over him.

'Cheers,' he said, getting out his pad

and writing her details down. 'So you moved in yesterday, then? I'm one of your neighbours. Live almost opposite, in fact. A very handy handyman!'

He kicked himself for his lame attempt at humour and quickly downed the last of his water, placing the glass back on to the kitchen counter. He didn't think it was wise to confess to being last night's failed visitor and this morning's over-eager surfer as well.

Sarah smiled politely. 'Come into the living room and I'll pay you.'

So that was it, he was getting his marching orders already. Well, the atmosphere was admittedly strained; he wanted to stay and leave, both at the same time.

Entering the living room, he couldn't help but notice the artistic arrangement on the table and the drawing pad sitting on the chair. Spontaneously he went over and looked at it. He wasn't an artist, but he could see that Sarah was no amateur. The way she had captured what were quite ordinary items and brought them to vivid life with detail and shading was incredible. He forgot his inhibitions for a moment.

'Wow, did you draw this today? It's amazing. Are you an artist?'

Sarah looked up from his invoice with a surprised expression on her face.

'Yes, I am.' He saw her struggle with her next words. 'By the way, I think we might have met on the beach early this morning.'

So, there it was, out in the open.

'Yes, I think we did,' Ben said, 'I was that incredibly over-intrusive surfer who followed you halfway up the beach with that bit of wood and the bag. presumably it was full of shells.' He pointed at the collection on the table. 'I'm sorry for interrupting your walk. I hope I didn't ruin your first morning on the beach.'

He saw Sarah's body begin to relax. Had he just started building a bridge between them, he wondered?

'No, it was very kind of you to do that. I'm the one who's sorry. I was

51

rude. You caught me at the wrong moment.'

He doubted that was entirely true. There was definitely something else going on that she wasn't saying. Even during his visit today, she had been decidedly frosty, except when her fiery side had kicked in when he'd caught her swearing at the boiler. The memory made the sides of his mouth start to twitch in amusement. He swallowed hard to control the chuckle that threatened to escape from his throat.

'That's okay,' he reassured her. 'We all have those moments.'

He started to move to the door but kicked something with his foot. Bending over, he picked up a shell.

'Oh, you dropped this,' he said placing it on the table. 'A mussel shell.'

'Yes, a blue mussel,' she informed him, her eyes unexpectedly brightening with enthusiasm and her guard dropping. 'It's mind-blowing to think that such a little thing feeds by filtering about eighteen gallons of water every

52

day. When you compare that to a human's two litres recommended intake . . . ' She trailed off and a dreamy look came over her face.

Ben was impressed. 'You certainly know your stuff,' he complimented her. 'Where did you learn that?'

'My father was a marine biologist. I spent more of my childhood by the sea or on the sea than at home.' She laughed wistfully and he listened with pleasure to the tinkling tones of her happiness. For a moment she looked like a different person, her face vibrant and youthful — as if she didn't have a care in the world.

'I expect he's looking forward to having lots of seaside holidays with you now you're living here,' he joked in response.

Her body suddenly stiffened and the tense atmosphere returned as if he had flicked a switch.

'He's dead.' she said abruptly. 'Cancer.' Breaking eye contact, she turned her back to him and started rummaging around in her purse. 'Here's your money.' She shoved some notes into his hand and strode over to the door, holding it open expectantly.

Taking his cue, Ben picked up his toolbox and walked towards her. He had clearly managed to upset her — again. Not knowing what to do for the best he followed, but at the door he paused briefly. 'I'm sorry to hear that,' he said. 'Anyway, get in touch if you need anything.'

There was no reply and as soon as both of his feet touched the doorstep, he heard the door click shut behind him, followed by the sound of two bolts being firmly drawn into place.

4

Ben spectacularly dived off his board and, limbs flailing, disappeared under the surf, not for the first time that morning. He surfaced, spluttering and blowing water out of his nose.

'Hey Benny-boy, been on the hard stuff last night?' Kai joked as he paddled past, ready to catch the next wave.

Ben shook his head in disgust. His track record over the last few days had been pathetic. He rubbed the sleepiness out of his eyes. It was another brilliant summer morning, just him and Kai with the whole ocean at their beck and call. It was a surfer's paradise, yet he had failed to ride one wave so far this morning.

He knew his mind had lost its usual focus over the last few days and his sleep was terrible. He was too hot, then too cold, then having strange, fuzzy dreams. He couldn't remember what happened in them but woke feeling disturbed and restless.

Ben thought back to when it had all changed. He kept replaying the meeting with Sarah on the shore and the next encounter at her cottage. Those blue eyes were etched on his brain, stunning him into distraction but also flashing with coldness, as if warning him to keep his distance. But that was the trouble; he couldn't stop thinking about her.

When he should have been concentrating on the surf, he was instead using the ocean as a vantage point, watching her cottage gate every day waiting for her to emerge into the wonders of the morning. He would lie on his board allowing himself to be carried up and down by the incoming waves which were gathering momentum but had yet to break and crash into the powerful Atlantic rollers that thundered towards the shore in a foam-showering beauty.

Ben would follow Sarah's path along

the beach as she explored the caves and rock pools then sifted amongst the tideline for her day's spoils. She'd finish her walk by making her way along the shore in the shallows, walking the mile or so back to the cottage. He'd watch her happily kicking her feet in the surf, looking lost in thought and glowing with beauty. He felt, guiltily, like some kind of stalker — yet he couldn't stop himself.

'Crikey dude, are you just going to lie there like some chick on an inflatable lilo or are you actually going to catch some waves today?'

Ben turned and saw Kai splashing towards him. 'Oh, man, you haven't got woman troubles, have you?'

Ben sighed. Kai sat up on his board and followed Ben's gaze inland. 'Hey, who's that?' he asked.

'My new neighbour,' Ben replied.

'She's an odd woman, if the grape-vine's right,' Kai said, glancing at her then turning his attention back to Ben. 'So, is Amy giving you an earful or have you heard from your ex?'

'No, it's fine,' Ben reassured him. 'Paula's long gone — moved to London with her new man if I've heard correctly, and Amy's behaving herself. I think I know how to handle her after all this time!' They laughed.

'Well, what's up then?' said Kai, 'You look like a drowned dog and I'm not even sure why you came surfing today. It's an ace day for it and you've barely ridden ten waves, and even then you've looked like a geriatric who had too much brandy for breakfast.'

Ben sighed. 'Have you ever thought you were content with your life, then some woman comes along and jams in your head like you're watching a DVD stuck on replay?' he asked.

Kai grinned. 'Ah, so it is a chick! Come on — details. Where did you meet her, what's her name, what's she like, did you get her number?'

'It's not that simple,' Ben said. He lapsed into silence and looked back at the shore. Sarah had stopped and was building something with the sand. *A true artist,* he thought.

'It never is,' Kai replied, then noticing Ben's distracted look, followed his line of vision. 'Not the new chick!' he exclaimed. He stared at Ben with a strange expression on his face. 'Oh, man, don't go there. That's not a good place to be, if the gossip's right.'

'Why?' Ben asked, but as he turned to look at Kai, a huge wave broke over them and he saw his friend paddling furiously then leap up on to his board and disappear in a blur of spray.

Ben spat out another lungful of salty water and struggled to collect his thoughts. What was so bad, and why? But by then Kai was heading back up the beach to his camper van and well out of reach.

Ben rebalanced himself on his board, lying there like a basking shark for a bit longer, the sea washing over him. He watched Sarah walk back to her cottage, then decided to call it a day himself.

It was still much earlier than he'd thought and he had plenty of time to kill before work. Dragging his board back up the beach, deep in thought, he couldn't resist taking a detour to take a look at Sarah's sand art.

He found it quite quickly, the waves almost ready to obliterate it from existence already. Kneeling down to have a proper look, he found she'd carved a beautiful fairytale castle out of the damp sand. He marvelled at its intricacy and how cleverly it had been constructed. She'd used tiny shells, strands of rope and small pebbles to add extra detail.

Oddly though, the second turret of the tower had caved in. As he looked more closely, he could see the remains were imprinted with the outline of some toes, as if it had been deliberately kicked down.

Ben shivered. Hastily he knocked the rest of the castle down with his fists. He wasn't sure why he'd done it. Looking back at the pile of sand, now being smoothed out by the surf, clouds obscured the sun for a few minutes and the day felt colder. He turned and ran towards home, suddenly desperate for a hot shower.

★ ★ ★

It was one of the warmest afternoons of the year so far. Sarah peeped out of her bathroom window. Small clusters of holidaymakers were gathered at the other end of the beach, near the main car park and the ice cream van.

Tiny children dressed in colourful sunhats ran around in the sand or sat quietly with their buckets and spades. Their parents lay gloriously sunbathing, reading or listening to their iPods, happy to find this little oasis on a lovely summer's day.

Sarah fingered the stretchy material of her swimsuit, enjoying its silkiness and wondered if she dared put it on. It had been a long time since she'd bared her body to anyone, let alone gone swimming.

She looked again, at her own end of

the beach this time. The sand lay empty and clear, beckoning her on to it for a clear, uninterrupted run down to the sea. Memories of teenage fun came back to her, spreading a smile over her face.

Sarah giggled to herself, stripped off her strappy T-shirt, navy cotton shorts and underwear then gently eased her swimsuit over her pale body. Catching her reflection in the mirror, she saw the fabric shimmering in the sunlight. A thrill ran down her spine. Picking up her multi-coloured beach towel, she wrapped it around her and made her way outdoors.

There was nowhere to hide her house key so she slipped it under an old sheet of corrugated iron that lay at the end of the garden and kicked some old plastic bags over it. The mess reminded her that when it was cooler, she would come out and start clearing away some of the debris.

The chaos of the house over the past couple of days had been irritating enough. A stream of home delivery vehicles had brought various bits of furniture, household appliances, art supplies and a huge stock of groceries. She hadn't been able to turn around without tripping over something that was waiting to be moved to a new home. She'd worked relentlessly into the small hours of every morning to restore calm and order to her environment. The unkempt garden stood out in stark contrast to the neatness inside.

Sarah made her way to the sea, nervously at first as she looked around her. The beach was still clear. As she got closer, the sound of the waves washing over the sand drew her away from the outside world. Throwing off her towel, she raced into the surf, gasping at first as the coldness hit her stomach, then she pushed her way out beyond the shallows and threw herself head first into the clean, pure water.

Enjoying the coolness of the ocean, Sarah surfaced and dived again. The weightlessness of the water held her body, allowing her to twist and tumble like a playful dolphin. The sea supported her every acrobatic move as she stretched her limbs in a state of blissful timelessness. The control and mastery she had over her body made her feel alive and nimble.

Sarah took an extra-large breath, sealed her lips and allowed her body to sink right down to the sea bed where she explored the gullies and sea life. When she had finished, she stretched back and floated on the soothing rhythm of the tide looking up at the clear blue sky. The moment held her in its soothing spell.

Her attention was recaptured by a shout, at the same time as a wave decided to break over her. Jerking upright and rubbing the salt out of her slightly stinging eyes, she trod water and looked towards the shore. Attached to her oversized towel was a small child who looked like she was trying to drag it home with her.

Sarah kicked her body flat and

headed towards the shore with a firm front crawl stroke. She sprinted up the beach, at the same time as a harried mother started running in her direction.

'Tegan, can you give that towel back? It's not yours, sweetie.' The mother called from some distance, looking hot and sweaty under the straw sunhat as she raced towards them.

The little girl dropped one corner of the towel then looked up with big innocent eyes at Sarah. She was no more than two years old, Sarah guessed, dressed in her Little Miss Sunshine T-shirt, matching yellow shorts, a floppy hat and jelly shoes.

'Are you a mermaid?' she asked Sarah in awe, her little voice clear but with a hint of shyness.

'No, I'm not a mermaid,' Sarah replied gently.

'Shiny colours,' the toddler said, pointing at the swimsuit.

Sarah laughed. 'My swimsuit does look like a mermaid's shiny tail but I'm not a mermaid,' she explained, 'I'm just a normal person.' But what was 'normal'? she wondered.

'Does your leg hurt?' asked the little girl. Sarah started. She looked down at the big, jagged, puckered scar on the top of her thigh that the child was pointing at. But at that moment, the mother arrived, breathless and flushed.

'I'm so sorry,' she said. Sarah took advantage of the distraction to pull her towel back and quickly wrap it around her before other prying eyes scrutinised her body. 'I took my focus off her for one minute and she was gone. I hope your towel is okay.'

'Yes, it's fine. It's not a problem.' Sarah smiled, feeling less exposed.

The mother turned to the child. 'Tegan, don't you go running off like that. And leave other people's stuff alone, too!'

'I thought the sea would drown it,' the child said indignantly, throwing her arms in the direction of the tide, which in fact was starting to come in.

Sarah glanced at the flustered mother and said to the toddler, 'That was very nice of you. I would have hated it if the sea had drowned my towel.'

The mother smiled kindly at her and Sarah felt a pang of loneliness. She watched as they walked back along the beach. This would never do; she was very happy being here by herself. Anyway, making friends would be too complicated, and complications were the last thing she wanted. She pulled the towel more tightly around her and headed home.

★ ★ ★

Ben looked at his newly repaired surfboard with satisfaction. Leaving it in the full heat of the sun had softened the old wax beautifully, making it much easier to scrape it off and replace it.

He ran his hand lovingly over the surface. It felt much stickier, much easier to ride and grip — that's if he actually managed to catch some waves instead of floating around on them in total distraction. Anyway, he'd spent all day managing to put those sort of thoughts out of his head and nothing was going to spoil the moment.

A clattering of tiny feet came up the driveway.

'Uncle Ben!' Tegan threw herself at his legs. He braced himself against the force then bent down, grabbed her and swung her round upside down as she squealed in delight.

'Tegan!' Amy puffed her way up the driveway behind her. 'What did I just tell you about running off?' She came to a halt beside Ben. He lowered Tegan to the floor, sensing his sister's unsettled mood. 'I've had a terrible day, topped off by this little rascal escaping from me on the beach and trying to run off with some swimmer's towel! It was extremely embarrassing but fortunately she was very good about it.'

'Mermaid,' Tegan said, trying to be helpful. 'Pretty mermaid.'

'You met a mermaid on the beach,

Princess?' Ben asked.

'Yes,' Tegan replied, 'Like my book.' She was referring to her favourite bedtime story, *The Little Mermaid*.

'And did she have long flowing locks and a big tail?' Ben teased.

'No,' Amy interrupted in an annoyed tone. 'She'd been enjoying a very nice swim like any human being then had to get back on the beach in double quick time to rescue her towel. Mind you, she was a pretty strong swimmer.'

'She had short brown curls and nice blue eyes.' Tegan added as she starting fiddling with Ben's block of wax.

He gently took it out of her little fingers as his forehead furrowed — the description sounded unsettlingly familiar. 'Did you meet her down the far end of the beach, by Shell Cottage?'

'Yes, that's right,' Amy said, 'near the rock pools.'

'Well, I think you might have just met our new neighbour. I've never heard her called a mermaid before, though!' Ben attempted to laugh off his discomfort.

Just as he'd been trying to forget about her, she had to pop up again. Was she trying to haunt him or something?

'Hurt leg,' Tegan piped up.

'You've hurt your leg?' Ben asked in concern.

'No, mermaid lady had. Big mark, like the one on mummy's tummy.' Tegan was referring to Amy's Caesarean scar.

'Yes, I noticed she had a nasty scar on her leg,' Amy said. 'Perhaps she's had a bad car accident or something. Anyway, Tegan, you need to get washed, then I'll make you some dinner.'

The twosome made their way inside.

Ben stood for a moment with even more questions going around in his head. Who was this woman nobody knew anything about, who was a very talented artist and had a serious scar. What's more, how did she get it?

5

Sarah carefully picked her way along the high tide line on a glorious Saturday morning in search of more interesting objects to draw. It had been a week now since she'd moved in, and her cottage was taking shape nicely. She was pleased with herself and felt she deserved her morning walk even more than usual.

She kicked aside another plastic bottle in disgust. She couldn't even understand the label which looked as if it was written in Russian. It pained her to think that sailors in big foreign ships treated the ocean as one big dustbin. Every day, the sea carried bottle after bottle on to the Cornish coastline. Through her father, she had become passionate about the issue of how dangerous and toxic plastic was to marine life. People just didn't understand the richness of the life beneath the ocean or how essential it was to their survival.

She'd used to be a driving force for many local beach clean-ups, persuading the locals to take a stand and care for their environment. *It would be great to do one here,* she mused, and then checked herself. Too many people, too many questions, she thought. Sad memories flooded through her body and she felt her bottom lip tremble.

'No, you are not going to let yourself think about that,' she firmly told herself out loud. 'This is a beautiful place to live and all you can control is your future. You're very lucky to be here at all.'

She turned her head into the wind, which was blowing off the sea, and imagined it catching all her unwanted thoughts and carrying them off to places where they would never be seen again.

Suddenly she felt weary after her days of hard work and sank on to her knees into the soft sand. It moulded to her body, nestling her in its embrace.

She scooped up some of the grains in her hands and watched them running finely through the gaps in her fingers. The wind snatched them away to find them a home on another part of the beach.

The salt of the ocean invisibly decorated her face, skin and hair. She licked her lips with pleasure, finding comfort in the familiar taste. She remembered all those days when her father had brought her home from an exhilarating day on the boat and her mother had grumbled as she'd tried to comb the tangles out of Sarah's hair.

She had always been closer to her father and was his precious only child. They'd shared a comfortable companionship, which had strengthened after her mother had died when Sarah was twenty-five.

Soon after, she'd married and there hadn't been any question at all about her father coming to live with them. He'd had his own annex, of course, and an independent life, but that still hadn't gone down too well with her husband. A tear rolled down her cheek. *Ex-husband,* she told herself bitterly. After all that had happened, and the consequences — which her father had suffered until he died — she wished she had never met him.

Sarah slammed her fists into the sand and felt her whole body shake with sadness and rage. She would never forgive him for everything he'd put her through. She just hoped it was definitely all over because she couldn't live that nightmare again. She'd covered her tracks as much as possible in an attempt to stop being hunted down. Hopefully she would succeed this time.

Raising her head, Sarah gazed out over the ocean, marvelling at its sheer size and radiance. The early morning sunlight skipped off the water, which sparkled like a million gemstones. She could see the swell of the waves as they steamed in from the Atlantic ocean.

Watching, she felt a thrill as their strength increased before that moment where they seemed to peak tantalisingly before crashing into a glorious crescendo of foam on their final sprint to the beach. Sarah's face relaxed as her body tuned into the sounds of the sea and calmed her down.

She spotted the lone surfer as he caught a massive wave and neatly rode his way along it, cleverly keeping his balance as it melded into a second wave, creating an even more powerful surge to the shore. From her position, she could see a big blaze of red on his chest and recalled that it was the wetsuit that the handyman, Ben, had been wearing when they first met. *He must be having his morning surf,* she thought. She'd noticed him quite often on her daily walks.

Her cheeks stung at the thought of their awkward first meeting and the irony of him turning up at her house later. It was as if somebody was trying to teach her a lesson, she thought in amusement.

And, if she was honest with herself,

he wasn't bad-looking either and his manner seemed gentle. She was surprised that he had dealt with her boiler outburst with sensitivity rather than calling her a typical female and implying that she couldn't cope by herself. She wasn't used to that sort of treatment from a man. Surely that had to count for something?

When she'd been struggling with some of her furniture, she'd wished that things had been different and she could have asked him to give her a hand. After all, he had offered. That's what she would have done in her old life, but things were different now.

It was just irritating that unwanted images of him kept popping into her head, even though she'd been trying to resist them by keeping herself busy.

Sarah sighed and drew a little heart in the sand, then finished it with an arrow. Getting up, she brushed the gritty grains off her knees and looked at her doodle with a wistful gaze on her face.

The next minute, her fantasy was quickly removed as a mixed ball of frustration and fear flooded through her body. Angrily, she bent back over to slash a big cross through the heart then kicked furiously at it with her bare foot, obliterating it from existence.

'Stupid woman!' she told herself. 'Stupid, stupid woman!'

★　★　★

Shaking the water out of his hair, Ben danced up the beach with a big grin on his face and his blood pumping wildly in his veins. It had been a fantastic morning for surfing and he'd faced the waves head on, catching them with perfect timing and controlling his board with exquisite precision.

'Benny-boy, you are back!' he told himself, punching triumphantly in the air with his fist and laughing at his boyish behaviour.

Later, after a hearty breakfast of fried bacon and eggs, Ben realised that he felt happier than he had in days. He still hadn't slept that well, having spent the night trying to piece together the information he had about Sarah and make sense of it all. The thrill of the morning's surf was exactly what he had needed to reignite his enthusiasm for life. He'd decided that everyone was entitled to hide their past.

His thoughts were interrupted by a knocking on the door. He could see the familiar red outline of the postman outside.

'Hello, Jago. Got something special for us today, have you?' Ben grinned at the regular postie.

'Well, it be a parcel for young Amy,' he said in a slow Cornish accent. 'I bet she's been going on that internet place again!'

They laughed. Jago handed the parcel and some other envelopes to Ben.

'Well, I'll have to tighten up the parental controls on the computer and put a limit on her credit card,' Ben joked. 'Thanks mate. Have a good day.'

As Jago started to move off, Ben noticed the name on the top envelope. 'Amanda Taylor, Shell Cottage'. That was strange. He knew that the new neighbour was called Sarah Daniels and before that Elsie had lived at the cottage for years. Someone must have got the wrong address, he thought.

'Hey, Jago!' Ben ran after the postman. Handing back the envelope, he explained, 'This isn't ours — it says it's for Shell Cottage. It hasn't got the new neighbour's name on it, though, and I don't know anyone else in the village called Taylor.' He examined the postmark and noted the quality of the envelope. 'It seems quite official too.'

The postman took a look. 'Oh, well, I've delivered another of these in that name over the last week. Are you sure there only be one maid living there?'

Ben thought for a moment. He hadn't seen anyone else . . . 'I don't think so. But I suppose if it's not for the cottage, then it'll be returned to the sender. No worries.'

He turned and walked back up the drive, his head spinning with another million and one questions. He was certain that nobody else had moved in and Sarah had always been alone when he'd seen her in the mornings, but why would she be receiving mail addressed to someone else? Did she have another female secretly living there, or was it simply a case of someone muddling up their addresses? Shell Cottage wasn't exactly an unusual name in these parts.

Ben hit himself on his forehead with the heel of his hand. Just as he had reconciled himself to staying out of Sarah's private life, more mysterious events happened. The most frustrating thing was that the more he found out, or couldn't figure out, the less he could let go of his ever-increasing attraction to Sarah.

'Benjamin, do you ever learn?' he scolded himself and decided that it was high time he fixed the leaky tap in the bathroom.

Sarah heard the clatter of the letterbox and a few letters landed on the mat. She didn't expect many. Very few people knew where she lived and she didn't think that many of those actually cared. She was just a name to them, someone they'd once known who wasn't part of their lives any more. She was happy for it to remain that way.

She leafed through the envelopes containing new customer information from the water and electric companies. All standard stuff and nothing that needed attending to yet, she thought, her mind already planning more productive things to do with the day ahead.

It was then that she noticed the stiff cream envelope and her fingers trembled. For a moment, she just stared at the address before she turned it over and slowly peeled it open.

★ ★ ★

One leaky tap, one creaky door and one toddler distraction later, Ben had managed to convince himself that someone must have mis-addressed the envelope. He mentioned it to Amy.

'Oh, it happens a lot. It's easy to believe that you know where someone lives so look up the address that you think it is and get it wrong. Shell Cottage, Beach Cottage, Sea View Cottage, you name it, there's heaps of them along this coast and easy to get mixed up, too. I mean, I think we'd have noticed if a second woman started coming and going from the house across the road, don't you?'

Ben agreed. His imagination was obviously working overtime and he must have been watching too many of Amy's Poirot programmes with her. Her explanation made the most sense.

'I'm off to the bakery then, Amy,' he announced. 'I've got your list but is there anything else you need?'

Satisfied he'd got his orders right, Ben absent-mindedly grabbed the closest shopping bag and headed out the door, his mind already wondering if he could slip a cream cake on to the bill without his sister noticing.

'Good morning, Ben.' The weathered woman in the bakery smiled at him warmly over the counter. 'What will you be wanting today?'

He asked for a white bloomer and a wholemeal loaf then gazed longingly at the array of cakes beaming happily at him from behind the glass counter.

'And be you wanting to slip in a little treat for your elevenses?' The woman gave him a friendly wink. 'Don't worry, I won't be spilling your secrets to the sister. My garden relies on your able hands since my back gave out on me.'

Ben's mouth watered. Decisions about food were not something that he found easy. He was torn between two of his particular favourites. Well, perhaps he could slip more than one into the bag.

'I'll have the chocolate éclair and the Chelsea bun, please,' he said with childish pleasure, 'But if Amy gets wind of this then I won't be left in any fit

83

state for gardening, or anything else for that matter!'

The whole queue erupted with laughter. Ben was popular with the villagers and they sometimes wondered why no girl had snapped him up yet. He was a natural with the ladies.

'I hear you're the only person who's met the new villager so far,' the woman commented. 'What's she like?'

Ben was surprised. He'd heard rumours that Sarah was a bit of a hermit but thought she would have at least made it to the local shops. He wanted to give a positive impression of her, but something told him to be a little guarded at the same time. 'Oh, she seems nice enough,' he said casually. 'I think she's been very busy trying to get the cottage shipshape this week. She didn't move in with much stuff.'

'So, is it just her, or is there a husband somewhere? Where has she moved from and why was she travelling so light?' The questions came firing at him from curious villagers.

'Um, I don't know. I only did a quick job for her.' Ben was economical with the details. He realised how little he did know about Sarah. The rest was constructed from random snippets of information and his imagination, which was not necessarily accurate.

Obviously, nobody else was much wiser. It was unusual in these close-knit parts to last more than a day before everyone knew your life history.

He opened his bag to put his goodies in and was aware from the chuckles around him that the focus had shifted away from Sarah. He soon realised why.

'Pink makes the boys wink!' a woman giggled. With his face matching the colour of his bag, Ben quickly handed over his money and did a runner, vowing to pay a bit more attention next time he snatched one of Amy's shopping bags in a hurry.

Ben decided to shortcut home across the beach. He had screwed the bag up as tight as it would go without squashing the bread but he still thought it shone like a beacon to everyone he passed. As much as he liked to think that he was in touch with his feminine side, this was taking things a bit far. He felt even more in need of a cake break now, and it would be better if he'd eaten at least one of them before he got home.

Shell Cottage looked pretty in the rays of the morning sun. The windows had been flung open and he could hear the sound of classical music drifting on the air. He fought the urge to stand and stare, forcing himself instead to look the other way at the outgoing tide. He noticed its calmness, ideal for the little boys who were playing with their toy boats, sailing them in the shallows with bits of string.

Just as he passed the cottage gate, his eyes still firmly on the children, he heard a loud wolf whistle behind him. His cheeks heated up again and he spun around. A group of teenagers laughed and ran off up the beach. He cursed silently to himself.

'Pink, eh? Poor guy. Are they teasing you?'

Ben recognised Sarah's voice. She giggled. He hadn't noticed her standing by the cottage gate, half-concealed by the overgrown hedge. Her dark green sleeveless T-shirt and black three-quarter length trousers had acted as a camouflage.

'It's all a terrible mistake,' he joked. 'I woke up this morning suffering from irreversible colour blindness and pink and blue look identical!'

He held his breath for a moment, not sure how she would respond to his attempts at humour. The gate hung between them like a protective barrier.

'Well, you'd better see if there's a pill for that because I don't want to think about what would happen if you went out on the surf in a pink wetsuit!'

Was it his imagination or did she blush slightly after her retort? Within seconds she was back to her usual distant self. 'Well, I need to get on with the gardening, so au revoir.' She moved away from him, shutting him off as quickly as she'd let him in.

But he wasn't ready to leave yet.

'What are you doing? Looks like you've been busy already today.' He'd spotted the large green gardening sacks bulging at the seams and the gardening gloves tossed on top of them.

She looked back while fiddling with something on the ground. He noticed her hesitate for a moment at his question. 'Just clearing away the chaos that seems to be growing wildly in my garden.' Her voice was semi-welcoming, as if she wasn't entirely sure whether she wanted to enter into a conversation with him or not.

'Ouch!' Sarah shot upright and held up a bleeding finger. Ben forgot his inhibitions and pushed open the garden gate, which promptly collapsed to one side on its sole hinge.

'Are you okay?' His voice was full of concern. 'What did you cut it on?'

'I'm fine.' Sarah stepped away slightly as he got closer. 'I just caught it on that wretched corrugated iron. I need to move it.'

'That's nasty stuff. Elsie used to have a shed here but it collapsed and everything got removed except the roof. Here, let me help you. I can borrow a van on Monday and take it to the tip, if you'd like. I really should have done it before you moved in, but there was so much to sort out and the garden got overlooked.'

Before Sarah had a chance to reply, he'd hung his bag on the gate post, pulled on the gardening gloves and was carefully lifting the sheet of metal away from its overgrown prison. He noticed her eyeing him with ambivalence. He realised that he was still quite a stranger to her and had just forced his way into her garden, her territory, and started taking over her work. If her relationship history was as bad as he suspected, then he wouldn't blame her if she threatened him with her shears.

'I'm sorry,' he said, in a belated attempt to make her feel more comfortable, 'I hope you don't mind me butting in and doing this. I can go, if that's what you want.'

She shifted awkwardly. 'It's okay, it's not the first time I've cut myself on it when I've been trying to move it. It's too big for me to manage really.'

Ben silently exhaled. He felt like he'd jumped the first hurdle. He suddenly felt braver. 'Those sacks look pretty heavy, too. I'm sure you can manage them but I can help you to shift them out the front and I'll take them away with this metal. It must be hard to organise these things when you're new to the area and don't have a van.'

Sarah wrapped a piece of tissue more tightly around her finger. She looked vulnerable just for a minute, and he had a strong urge to reach out and embrace her in his strong arms.

'Yes, that would be nice. Thank you.' Her voice stuttered a bit. 'It is difficult. Excuse me, I need to go inside and put a plaster on this.' She retreated into the cottage.

Ben felt an exciting warmth well up inside of him. Something had altered between them. Sarah was obviously worried about him being there but seemed to be starting to accept him. He was irresistibly attracted to her, drawn to her enigmatic nature and ever-changing emotions. There was a flirty edge to her humour and a strength to her character, yet her sensitivity and fear made her put up barriers at every turn. He wanted to find out more, yet he was aware that he could be entering dangerous territory.

Sarah came back out into the garden, complete with a pair of bright pink gardening gloves on her hands.

'I thought I'd better put these on and give you some help. That's a big sheet of metal and it might be easier with two of us. Of course, we could always swap gloves if you want!'

Ben felt the rest of the tension between them evaporate.

'Sounds great. You start at the top and I'll keep going with this corner. We won't let bindweed defeat us!'

They laughed in unison and set to work. Ben mentally constructed safe topics of conversation to keep them going: the sea, gardening, what she was going to do to the cottage and funny tales about his work. He was careful not to ask prying questions about her life.

'One step at a time,' he told himself mentally. 'One step at a time.'

★ ★ ★

Two hours later, Sarah stepped back and wiped the sweat off her face with a dirty hand. The corrugated iron and bags of garden waste were sitting out at the front ready to be disposed of, the gate was swinging on two hinges and Ben had also helped her to trim the highest bits of the hedge with its thick branches. She was grateful that he had turned up when he did. Her finger still throbbed.

'Well, I think that's as far as we can get today,' she said. She checked herself; had she implied that 'we' could do some more another day? She hoped not, though secretly wondered what it would be like to see him again.

'Yes, that was a good morning's work. Very satisfying.' Ben stretched. 'Oh, my poor muscles! I don't suppose you could spare a glass of water too? I'm parched.'

Sarah smiled to herself. Ben reminded her a bit of her father when he'd used that last expression.

'Well, we can't have you being parched,' she said teasingly. 'Give me a minute to go and get us a drink.'

She returned with two glasses of ice-cold water.

Ben eyed up the bag on the gatepost. 'Um, I bought myself two cakes this morning but that was a tad greedy of me. Would you like to share?'

Sarah's stomach had been rumbling for a while and she knew that he'd heard it. 'That's a lovely idea, but let's go and sit on the beach. Much better than this garden,' she said. She didn't want him to leave just yet but felt a bit threatened by the idea of them sharing cake in her garden.

'Okay, but if anyone spots the pink bag, I'm pretending it's yours!'

Sitting on the sand, minutes later, he rummaged around in the offending bag. 'Right, I've got an éclair and a Chelsea bun. The choice is yours.'

'I don't mind,' Sarah replied politely.

'Well, I know how women like their chocolate so the éclair seems to have your name written all over it.' Ben handed it to her with a grin.

She suspected that he had a secret craving for the éclair himself, and was touched by his generosity.

'It might be a bit melted in this heat so you'd better have the napkin that goes with it.' Ben picked it up and reached over to her. Her skin tingled in the close proximity of his masculine smell. For a brief second their fingers touched and they looked at each other in silence. Transfixed, she found herself sinking deep into his hazel eyes. Her heart pounded in her ears and she wanted to both draw away and stay locked in this scene forever.

'Sarah,' Ben began to speak in a soft voice.

Suddenly, she felt sick and drew back, breaking the moment. 'Thank you for all your help today, Ben, it's been great. And it was very kind of you to share your éclair but I think I'll save it for later.' She shoved it into the brown paper bag, picked up the empty glasses and pushed herself to her feet.

'Sarah, what's wrong?'

She forced herself to look at him, still torn. His gentle concern touched part of her soul that had lain dormant for a long time. Her heart ached.

'Perhaps I can come back tomorrow to help clear some more stuff from the garden,' he said hopefully. 'I might as well go to the tip with a full van and the weather's in our favour at the moment.'

Sarah paused. She knew what she wanted, but was it right? She sensed his attraction to her but wasn't confident that she should encourage him. Her thoughts were shattered when a tiny voice cried out.

'This is where you're hiding!' A shower of sand sprayed everywhere as a child skidded to a halt and threw herself on to her knees. Ben looked at her and held out his arms for a big hug.

'Hello, Tegan, what are you doing here, Princess? Where's Mummy?'

'We were waiting for you to come home. Then you didn't. Mummy said we should go and find you.' Tegan chattered on, oblivious to the situation she'd just interrupted.

Sarah noticed the love shining from his eyes as he looked at the child who shared his identical brown hair and dimpled cheeks. She stood, shocked. Looking up, she spotted an attractive woman strolling towards them. She recognised her immediately. Pain stabbed at her insides and she knew she had to get out of there.

'Ben,' she interrupted, 'I've got to go. You don't need to come back tomorrow. It'll be fine. Thanks, though.'

She quickly turned and hurried up the garden path so he couldn't see the

96

tears that threatened to roll down her face. She was a fool, expecting him to be single. She was looking for something that didn't even exist and there was no way she was going to be used and hurt again.

Sarah slammed the back door shut, angry with herself for feeling forbidden emotions. She shot the bolts into place then furiously threw the chocolate éclair across the kitchen. It hit the wall with a thud and slid down to make a creamy mess on the lino.

6

Ben stopped at the end of the drive and gazed at the cottage: It had been over a week since the episode on the beach. His brow creased as he replayed it over and over again in his head. Things had been going so well, then it was as if the scene had frozen over. Was Sarah really that ambivalent about meeting other villagers?

'Ben, what's up?' Amy appeared on the doorstep. 'You're not still looking at the cottage, surely?'

He'd been standing there for most of the week, or staring out of his bedroom window. When he'd gone back on Monday to collect the garden waste, there had been no sign of Sarah and she hadn't responded to his knocks. The windows and doors had been closed day and night. No lights shone at the windows when dusk fell. It was worrying. He hadn't even seen Sarah on a morning walk, though the high tide was getting later so his surfing times had changed. He hoped that she was okay.

'Just seeing if there's any sign of life.' Ben attempted to remain casual, but his tone had a melancholy edge. He was tired and his head ached. The bright sunlight was blinding and sent stabbing pains deep into his brain. He rubbed at his watery eyes.

'Well, maybe she went away for a few days,' Amy pondered. 'Though a home delivery van went in yesterday while you were at work so she must be there. She's not starving to death. Don't worry, it's none of our business anyway. She's only a neighbour.'

Ben struggled with Amy's offhand comments. He sensed that she was fed up with him moping around.

On the surface, he knew that Sarah was 'only a neighbour' and, after all, he'd merely done a few jobs for her. That didn't make him her keeper and protector. She kept haunting his mind, though — her blue eyes exposing a tender vulnerability and her slender beauty melting into his arms in his dreams. He knew that he should let go and get on with his own life. If only it were that easy.

Ben's headache intensified and something broke inside him, releasing days of pent-up heartache.

'Since when did you become so uncaring?' Ben snapped back, without thinking. 'She's a single woman living on her own and I don't think she's had an easy life. How would you have felt if everyone had abandoned you after what happened with Tim? I even moved in with you! Sarah, on the other hand, doesn't seem to have anyone. And you want me to forget about her as if she's not a human being with the same feelings as everyone else?'

As soon as the words came out, he wished he could take them back. Amy's eyes shone with hurt and she bit her lip.

'Amy, I'm sorry.' Ben moved towards her.

'Sorry? And that makes it all right? I didn't mean to sound cruel. I just get the impression that our presence is unwelcome and she would prefer us to keep our distance, that's all. I don't want you getting involved in rescuing another woman and feeling tied to her as well.'

'Amy, I don't feel tied to you. I love you and I'm happy living here. It's my sanctuary too. And how could I live without your home baking?' Ben softly teased her, bringing a wobbly smile to her face.

'Hey, come here.' He gave Amy a big hug. 'You're my sister and you're the best one I could ever have.' As she buried her face into his broad shoulder, Ben noticed a curtain twitch from the bedroom of the cottage. He peered closely. Sarah was standing there motionless looking at both of them. It was then he realised why she might have run away. He felt cold to the pit of his stomach. Was it too late to put things right?

* * *

Sarah dug her nails into the palm of her hand until half-moon shapes traced painfully across her skin. Seeing Ben hold another woman like that, slowly taking her into the comfort of his arms, ripped into her.

She didn't know why she had kept watching. Perhaps to remind herself that she had to let go and forget someone who was totally unavailable to her. It was only her own longing that had misinterpreted his friendliness as something more. She didn't think he was so brazen as to try to have a mistress so close to home.

Sarah was angry with Ben for leading her on, but deep down she knew that she was the one who was to blame. It had been so long since a man had flirted with her that she had misread the signs. She kicked the skirting board in disgust and a rotten sliver of wood dropped on to the carpet.

Great, she thought, *more cleaning up*

to do. She realised that she couldn't cope with being cooped up indoors any more. She needed fresh air to clear out her lungs and sweep away the cobwebs in her head. For days she had sat in front of her canvas trying to absorb herself in a stunning coastal scene, but it still looked flat and uninspiring.

She decided to take her camera and head off along the coast path. The light was just right now it was early afternoon, losing its uncomfortable glare that had the potential to over-expose her shots.

Sarah walked across the beach, giving a wide berth to the families that had scattered themselves over the sand. They'd have to move soon anyway, she reasoned, with the tide on the turn, and then she'd have a clear run back. All she craved was to be alone with the comforting sounds of the ocean to soothe her soul. The wind ruffled her hair, giving a youthful freshness to her face. Sarah smiled. It would be okay, she told herself, she just needed to focus on her art and forget about Ben. Nothing had happened and nothing would happen. She should be grateful for that. It saved a lot of potential complications.

★ ★ ★

Ben yanked the zipper of his wetsuit upwards with too much force. It jammed, causing him to swear loudly. He twisted around like a bendy man in an attempt to free it and lost his balance, falling on to the sand.

'Hey, you okay, dude?' Kai appeared and looked down with concern.

'This damned zip!' Ben swore repeatedly and got up.

'Sounds like you're having a bad day, mate.' Kai said, dropping his board and manipulating Ben's zip back into position, then pulling it up to his neck. He patted him on the back. 'There you go.'

Ben gasped as the twisted rubber neck threatened to cut into his throat.

He shoved his finger into the suit and pulled it straight. His head was able to move, that was an improvement, he thought.

Maybe that was the problem, his head had been so focused on Sarah lately that he'd forgotten to look at the other positive things in his life like being an uncle — and his next surfing competition.

'Let's go and catch some waves,' he said. 'I need a distraction.'

Kai thought twice about asking any more questions. 'Yes mate, let's go. Nothing like a good surf to sort things out.'

The pair of them headed off to the ocean. Just as Ben got to the shallows, he noticed Sarah making her way back down the cliff path. He stood there for a moment.

'You go on in, I'll follow.'

He wondered if it was a good time to talk to her. The water curled itself around his feet, washing the sand over them as if encasing them in a plaster cast. He shook his toes free before he sank deeper but his mind was on other things. Even if Sarah did come close to him, what would he say? It wasn't as if anything had developed between them yet, although he'd been so close to hinting at his attraction last week before Tegan had interrupted.

Sarah didn't look at him as she traipsed past, even though there were only four surfboard lengths between them.

Ben felt his heart racing faster and faster. He paused then took a deep breath. 'Sarah,' he called. 'Have you got a minute?'

★ ★ ★

She had seen him, as soon as she'd got to the top of the cliff path. It was hard to miss the only surfer she knew with red logos all over his suit. His delay had frustrated her. She needed him to get into the sea and out of her way. Finally, she had descended back on to the beach. It was irritating how he was poised in the shallows like a tiger waiting for the kill. She was determined that he wasn't going to have any more of her blood. Looking deliberately inland, she marched resolutely past him. Nothing would make her stop, nothing.

There was a second shout.

'Sarah, hold on. Please. We need to talk.'

Her body stiffened and she walked faster. Only a few more minutes and she'd be in the safety of her home, where he couldn't touch her.

He cried out again but it was different this time. A blood curling howl that tore through the air. Sarah instinctively turned and saw him collapse on to the sand, screaming and clutching his foot. She ran towards him.

Kai reached Ben at the same time as Sarah, his face ashen. 'Ben, what's wrong?' He stared at Ben's crumpled body which was shaking with pain, then up at Sarah.

She took one look at Kai, still standing in the shallows and noticed a quick movement near his feet. 'Stop!' she said, thinking fast. 'Don't move! Take a big step and get out of the sea in one go. Weaver fish!'

Kai didn't hesitate, taking a huge jump to the safety of the shore.

'Ben, you've stepped on a weaver fish. We have to treat you fast.' She turned to Kai. 'Can you help me to move him? We need to get him back to my cottage as quickly as possible.' As she scooped her hands under Ben's armpits, she said, 'Have you had weaver fish here before?'

Kai deposited the two surfboards further up on the beach then came back and helped her to lift Ben, taking most of the weight on his shoulders. Sarah was grateful as Ben was limp and heavy.

'No, never come across one,' he gasped.

As they half carried, half dragged Ben into the living room, Sarah speedily recapped on her knowledge of weaver

108

fish and dashed off to fill a large bucket with water. Kai carefully peeled Ben out of his wetsuit and wrapped him in one of Sarah's blankets.

'Ben,' she said urgently on her return, 'Listen to me. I'm going to put your foot in some very hot water. It will hurt but it will get the poison out and save you a lot of pain in the long run. Is that okay?'

He groaned and nodded, his eyes glazed in agony as his foot was lowered into the bucket. Kai studied him with worried eyes.

'Ben will be okay,' Sarah reassured Kai. 'Can you tell his wife?'

Kai looked blankly at her. 'Ben doesn't have a wife,' he said.

'Well, girlfriend then,' Sarah was curt. 'The woman he lives with!'

'Oh, that's his sister, Amy, and her little girl. Ben's not with anyone at the moment,' Kai replied. 'Amy's in Truro tonight with her mum but I'll pass on a message. Are you okay from here? I need to grab the boards and I'll get some clothes for Ben too.'

Sarah was stunned. His sister? Everything cleared before her eyes. Goodness, she was an idiot.

'Yes, I'm fine,' she said. 'He shouldn't need hospital treatment. I can take care of it. I've dealt with plenty of these injuries before.'

As Kai disappeared, she looked at Ben. His head lolled back on the chair as shards of pain shot up his leg. He looked like a helpless little boy. Filled with emotion, she put her hand on his head and stroked his coarse hair.

'There, there,' she murmured. 'I know it hurts but it'll get better soon, it will. Don't worry.'

She gazed at him with compassion in her eyes and, in semi-consciousness, he clutched her other hand, gripping it as if holding on for dear life. As they sat together in silence, taking comfort from one another's presence; Sarah wanted this moment to last forever.

Sarah remained kneeling on the floor holding Ben's hand for a few hours, regularly changing the water and having to experience the guilt caused by seeing a fresh wave of pain shoot through him. She hated hurting him but knew that it would make things better.

His breathing was less shallow and the colour was starting to return to his white cheeks as she watched over him for almost the whole day. Just as the evening sun disappeared behind the trees, she noticed Ben open his eyes.

'Did I stand on a needle or something?' he asked groggily.

'No, no,' she said. 'It was a weaver fish, but don't worry, you're coming along nicely and you should be fine soon.'

'Weaver fish?' he asked in surprise. 'What's one of those?'

'It's a tiny devilish fish that hides just under the sand. It pokes its spine up ready to inject oodles of venom into any poor person who stands on it,' Sarah explained. 'The hot water should have got most of the poison out but it'll be sore for a while. You'll probably find it better if you take some painkillers and stay off your feet, though.'

Ben groaned. 'Little critter. It's really painful!'

Sarah was relieved that he was starting to talk. In rare cases, people had died of respiratory failure following weaver fish stings and his slow breathing earlier had alarmed her. She'd kept her phone nearby in case she needed to dial for help.

'But how does scalding my foot in a bucket of water help?' Ben asked. 'It just makes it hurt more!'

'The hot water is very clever. It breaks down the poison and it also helps blood to flow to your foot. That means it can naturally cleanse and heal itself. I don't think weaver fish are too partial to having massive great human feet clomping all over them,' Sarah teased him.

'Well, I think the fish got its revenge.' Ben grimaced, shuffling himself into a more upright sitting position. He wiggled his foot in the water.

'It's not feeling so bad now, actually. Perhaps you do have a point after all. You are my knight-ess in shining armour.' He laughed and dodged a half-hearted blow from her cushion.

Sarah felt a wave of shyness wash over her at her boldness. 'Um, if you don't mind, I just want to take a look at your foot. Check that the fish didn't leave any of its spines behind.'

He lifted his foot on to the towel on her knee. She looked at its redness and gently patted at the swollen skin to dry it a little. He winced.

'Sorry,' she said, carefully caressing his heel in her hand and peering at the sole. He was like a little lamb, she thought, allowing her to manipulate his limb even though it must still be hurting quite a bit.

There was no sign of anything in his foot. 'All clear,' she announced, easing his foot back into the bucket. 'You'll live to see another day.'

'That's a relief! I'm not ready to go yet.' The atmosphere shifted as he added in a more serious tone, 'There's still so much I want to do.'

She realised it was time to clear the air.

'Ben,' she said at the same time as he uttered her name.

They hesitated, unsure about who should go first. She drew a deep breath. 'Ben, I'm sorry about the other day. Kai told me that Amy is your sister. I got my wires crossed and thought she was your wife. It was rude of me to walk off like that. I had no reason to.'

'No, I'm the one who should be apologising,' he said. 'I should have told you before. I'm so used to my living arrangements that I don't think about how they would look to a stranger.' He blushed. 'Not that I mean you're a stranger of course — but you know what I mean.'

Ben stopped as if to choose his next words carefully. She waited in anticipation. Finally he spoke. 'I think we were both aware of what almost happened before Tegan gate-crashed our mini picnic. Well, that's if you were thinking along the same lines as me . . . perhaps you weren't, in which case it might have been better if that fish had finished me off.' He laughed awkwardly. 'I'm rambling now!'

She felt sorry for him. 'No,' she said, with more confidence than she felt. 'I think we had similar thoughts.' Her stomach tightened.

Their eyes met in a moment of shared understanding and he started to bend forward. For some reason, she didn't feel scared any more. Her heart beat faster as he paused for a moment then she shut her eyes in anticipation. His lips touched hers and longing flooded through her body.

Sarah kissed him back with softness and desire. In the comforting warmth of the summer evening, nothing seemed to matter any more.

Ben responded to Sarah's passionate kiss with equal fire, as if he'd been starved of love for far too long. He pulled her on to his lap and they sat there enjoying one another with a gentle tenderness. He slid his strong arms around her petite body, unable to believe that it was really happening and that she hadn't slapped him for his behaviour. A troubling image shot into his head and he abruptly pulled back.

'Sarah, are you sure this is right for you?'

She looked at him, her face flushed with pleasure and her blue eyes stirring his emotions more strongly this time. Without replying, she rested her hand against his cheek and gave him another long kiss. She straightened up.

'Thank you,' she said.

'Thank me for what?' Ben asked with confusion.

'For caring. And — ' her voice trailed off.

'And what?' he asked but she was already lifting herself off his knee, avoiding his question. Her voice slipped back into her nurse-like manner.

'How's the pain? Are you ready for something to eat? I'll get you some painkillers and you can get dressed.' She pointed at the carrier bag which Kai had left on the settee.

So was that it? Had the old practical distant Sarah returned? Ben felt space flood between them. 'Yes, food would be great. Thanks.' Could he pretend that nothing had just happened?

'Sarah?' She was just starting to leave the room, but stopped and looked at him. 'Are we okay?' Ben's voice wobbled.

She looked at him for a minute. He found it impossible to read her expression, then the corners of her mouth twitched in a semi-smile.

'Yes, it's okay. It's just . . . complicated, that's all.'

'It doesn't have to be,' Ben said, 'We can take things slowly.' He wasn't prepared to lose her now but also didn't want to come across as desperate and possessive. He wanted her to feel in control; to slowly learn to trust him.

'Perhaps,' she said. 'Anyway, I need to put dinner on. I'm sorry to ask this, but is fish okay?'

They both laughed and Ben felt some of the ice melt. He'd do whatever he needed to win Sarah's heart and nothing was going to get in his way.

7

Ben lifted his foot out of the bucket, then, having mischievous second thoughts, put it back in. 'Sarah, would you be able to sort out my foot so that I can sit up to the table to eat?' he called. The sound of chopping stopped and she came back in.

'Oh no, is it too swollen for you to reach it comfortably?' she asked in concern, grabbing a low stool and sitting by him. Spreading the towel over her knees again, she slowly eased his foot on to her lap and patted it dry. The lightness of her touch was comforting on his skin.

'It's still looking quite pink but that's normal. I expect it feels quite heavy and achy,' she commented. 'Oh, I forgot the painkillers.'

She returned with a glass of water and two pills, catching him closely examining his foot and sporting a cheeky grin on his face.

'If I didn't know better, I'd suspect that you just made up that story to get your hands on me once more,' she said in mock sternness, placing her hands on her hips and comically glaring at him.

'Me?' he exclaimed with a big innocent expression, perfected by spending plenty of time with Tegan.

Sarah put the water and pills down on the table out of his reach. 'Right, well, if you're feeling that much better then you can hobble over and reach your own pills, and then clear my bits and pieces off the table for dinner. You can put it all in that box on the chair.' She pointed to the chair.

Ben pulled himself upright, his foot the size of a balloon but not feeling as sore as it looked. That was a relief. He threw on his clothes then limped over to the table and swallowed the pills. Next, he set about clearing away the beachcombing spoils and art stuff that covered the table. He had nearly finished when his foot burned painfully and he lost his balance, knocking Sarah's sketch pad to the floor.

'Are you okay?' she shouted from the kitchen.

'Yes, yes, just lost my balance. I'm fine,' he replied bending over to scoop up the loose papers that had dropped out. He noticed that Sarah had drawn on many of them and couldn't resist having a look. He'd seen an example of how talented she was before and was keen to admire more of her work. He spread the drawings out on the table and bent over them. Shocked, he studied the intense dark colours and sharp abstract images that screamed out at him from the paper. He looked at the other drawings and saw more and more of the same.

Ben felt a chill rushing through his veins at the unhappiness depicted in the drawings. He felt like he was snooping into something that was intensely private and never intended for anyone else's eyes.

'How are you going in there? I'm

going to serve up in a few minutes,' Sarah called, breaking into his thoughts.

Starting like a naughty child who'd almost been caught in the act, Ben hastily gathered together the papers and put them back in the art pad, firmly burying it in the box and moving it on to the floor in the corner of the room. He wished that he'd never looked.

'Er, yes, just finished,' he shouted back in the most relaxed voice he could manage under the circumstances. 'I'm just going to pop to the bathroom first though.'

He needed some time to gather his thoughts before he had dinner with the woman who held him under her spell, yet had perilously unchartered depths. Despite his niggling concerns, he felt impelled to keep exploring.

'Am I being a fool?' he asked himself out loud, looking at his reflection in the bathroom mirror. 'Or should I persevere and win over the woman that I think I've fallen in love with?'

The mirror gazed back in silence.

Ben realised that there was no right answer. It depended on his willingness to take the plunge and find out what lay beneath the waters.

★ ★ ★

Sarah dropped a splodge of mashed potato on to the plate. Her whole body still reeled slightly from the enormity of what had just happened. She couldn't believe that she was actually doing this, that she'd just kissed Ben and was going back for more.

Her head cried out that she was stupid and heading for disaster, yet her heart longed for this afternoon to be the start of something beautiful, as if the past had never existed and she could be like any normal, untainted, lover. She yearned to lie in his strong arms and rest her head on his muscled chest, taking solace in the rhythmic beating of his heart and feeling safe.

Is this what it's all about though, she asked herself, *needing another person to feel safe?* That sounded, quite frankly, dangerous. She'd spent so much time over the past two years erecting and building impenetrable protective barriers around her life and soul. Sarah had learned that nobody could be trusted. Even people she had thought she could depend on turned against her in doubt. When she had most needed support and loyalty, there had only been hostility and judgements.

She had desperately missed the solid presence of her father, even though he hadn't been strong enough to fight her corner when he was alive. They had both been devastated when he'd been diagnosed with cancer. *He might have survived it,* she thought bitterly, *if he'd been given the chance.*

If I'd given him a chance, she thought, thrusting her spoon angrily back into the potato saucepan.

She thought of his death and felt guilty. She'd always wondered if he would have survived if she'd made a different decision. The consequences of her choices and actions would haunt her forever. Physical scars were nothing compared to the emotional ones.

And now Ben was on the scene and it didn't look as if he was going to leave her alone in a hurry. Not that she wanted him to. It was going to be a tricky path to navigate and she just hoped that he'd never find out what he was taking on or he'd run a mile.

The beeping of the oven timer brought her attention back to the meal. Grabbing the fish, she slid it on to the plates and, gathering her courage, carried them into the living room.

★ ★ ★

Sarah watched as Ben scraped the last of his food off the plate and swallowed it with an appreciative sigh.

'That was delicious,' he said, 'I could eat seconds, thirds and fourths! Where did you learn to cook fish like that?'

Sarah felt a happy warmth fill her body. It had been a long time since someone had complimented her on her cooking. She had forgotten what it felt like, giving someone satisfaction through her own efforts.

'Like I said, I spent most of my childhood on a boat. My father often caught fish and my mother had plenty of practice in cooking it to perfection. I often helped her in the kitchen. I find cooking very relaxing and fun.'

She saw Ben start to open his mouth as if to ask her something else. She jumped in quickly to forestall any difficult questions. 'So, tell me about your sister and her little girl. How did you end up living with her?'

'Oh, that's a long story,' Ben said. 'We both had relationships that ended badly and she was struggling a bit as a single mother. I needed somewhere to live and she wanted some support so we both ended up helping each other, really.'

Sarah suspected that he had chosen his words carefully. The affected casual-ness of his reply was betrayed by his fingers fiddling nervously with the stem of his wine glass. She decided to move on to safer ground. 'Your little niece looks very cute. How old is she?' Complimenting a child was always a good move.

'Tegan? She's just two years old but already giving us a hint of what she could be like as a teenager! Mind you, time goes so quickly that by the time she's grown out of the terrible twos, she'll be growing into the torturous teens and giving her mother more nightmares.' They both laughed.

'Yes, who would be a teenager again?' Sarah shuddered. 'All the turmoil of first love, finding your identity and sitting exams. I hated exams!'

'Me too,' Ben agreed. 'But I wish I'd appreciated how easy school was compared to going to work. I do love my job, but standing on a ladder in strong winds because some old dear can't live without their television for a few hours isn't my idea of fun.' He paused. 'Anyway, how about you — have you always been an artist?'

Sarah felt on familiar territory.

'Yes and no. I started drawing when I was little but I also wanted to be a teacher, professional show jumper, actress and nurse, as children do! Art was something that I came back to when I was at college and it suited my lifestyle later on when I needed to work from home.' She hoped that he wouldn't ask why. In a hurry, she added, 'It's great living here. All the scenery and beautiful things to draw and paint. And the light is amazing, just perfect for artists. How about you? Is surfing your true love?' She checked herself. Why had she used that particular expression?

He grinned, his dimples lighting up his face.

'Surfing is incredible,' he said, 'When I'm out there on that board it's simply amazing. I've surfed since I was a nipper and do lots of competitions too. I can't imagine ever living far away from the sea. I'd feel like I was missing an essential part of myself.'

'I know what you mean,' Sarah added with enthusiasm, her voice taking on a new life. 'Being at one with nature is the most fulfilling experience. It makes me feel whole, complete, somehow. I never stop marvelling at how clever nature is. We'll never stop learning new things about it. I feel so humble when I think about how small we are in comparison to the wonders that take place around us every day.'

Ben's nodded vigorously.

'It's great to meet someone who feels passionately about it, too. Amy's so caught up in her work and motherhood I'm not sure she even appreciates the natural beauty around her.' He leaned forward and looked straight into Sarah's eyes. She twisted her napkin nervously as she waited in anticipation for his next comments. 'One thing, though. As much as surfing is my life, I would never describe it as my true love. I think that label should always be reserved for someone special.' His voice dropped, sending tinglings down her spine. 'And true love usually pops up when you least expect it.'

Sarah trembled, wanting more but not daring to hope for it. She wasn't sure what to say next.

Ben pushed his plate aside and lifted up his dessert bowl, placing it in the middle of the table. 'This chocolate cake looks delicious,' he said, twiddling a fork in his hands. 'But I think the lady should try it first.'

Without waiting for an answer, he sliced off a corner and smoothly moved it to her lips. The sweet taste of the chocolate lingered in her mouth then slipped down her throat. 'Yes, it's good,' she whispered.

'Hush,' he said, placing a finger on her lips. Moving beside her, he took her hands in his and pulled her into his arms. The air crackled for a moment before he enfolded her in his warmth and sent her emotions dizzy with his passionate kiss.

Sarah abandoned her reservations and kissed him back with equal hunger.

She realised that she was hopelessly, head over heels, in love with Ben, even though she knew that any relationship would end up causing them both intense pain.

At that moment though, she didn't care. All she wanted was Ben.

8

Ben woke up on Sarah's couch. For a moment he couldn't remember where he was. Light was pouring in through the living room window and he could hear the sound of a shower running.

Memories of last night returned to him. He stretched out with a big smile on his face. It had been late by the time he had finished kissing Sarah and then she'd fallen asleep in his arms. He'd spent hours just gazing at her. She'd looked peaceful, with a sweet vulnerability. He'd softly stroked her face which glowed with love and happiness.

Thoughts of her artwork flashed back at him and he wondered how anyone could so badly hurt someone as beautiful and gentle as Sarah. He'd been careful to keep his passion reined in, sensing that he needed to take things slowly with her, but wanting far more.

He knew that it would take time for her to reveal her secrets, but he was more than willing to wait.

He realised that after he'd eventually fallen asleep himself, Sarah must have woken when it got colder and gone to bed. He cuddled himself in the red fleece blanket that covered him. Closing his eyes, he wondered what the day ahead would hold.

He felt slightly nervous, like a teenager on a first date. It had been a while since he'd met anyone who'd had such an effect on him as Sarah.

'Hello, stranger, you're awake at last then.' Sarah was standing there smiling through the door at him. Her curly hair was still wet from the shower and made her glisten in the morning sunshine. He took in the slender curves of her body, her petite waist emphasising her hourglass figure.

He was tempted to offer to teach her to surf, but then remembered Tegan's tales about Sarah's scar and didn't want to make her feel awkward. *Perhaps one day*, he thought, *perhaps one day*. Was he thinking about a future for them already? He realised that he couldn't see one without her. Sarah's trust in him last night had made him feel special and he wanted to protect her, give her the life she deserved.

'How's the foot?'

Ben brought himself back to the present and stuck his injured limb in the air. He carefully stretched out his foot and wiggled his toes.

'Well, it seems to be about half the size that it was yesterday and I slept okay — so either the painkillers worked or your magic touch has produced a miracle cure.' He laughed impishly. 'Any chance of you checking it over for me, just to update me on its progress?'

He waited with trepidation. How would Sarah respond to him this morning? So far the vibes felt good but perhaps she was just being friendly. But she entered the room and perched on the arm of the couch. 'Looks okay to me,' she said, smiling. 'Come on then, lift it up and let Nurse Sarah have a peek.'

Ben obediently placed his foot in her lap, enjoying the sensation of her fingers deftly examining his foot. 'Yes, it's healing very well. Yesterday I said you'd live to see another day. Today I predict that you'll live a full and happy life.' She fixed her blue eyes on him, adding, 'But I don't recommend that you dice with any more weaver fish. It could have been much worse and needed medical attention, which would mean needles and minor surgery.'

He winced. 'Ouch! Lucky I had you, then.'

'I'm going to make us some breakfast,' Sarah said. 'You can use the bathroom now if you want.'

He gently grabbed her wrist as she made to go, spinning her round to face him. 'Sarah, I just wanted to ask. I mean, is everything okay? You don't have any regrets?' He felt her tremble slightly.

'No,' she replied. 'No regrets.' She

squeezed his hand affectionately, sending a warm glow through his body. 'Go and shower, then we can eat.'

He started to pull her towards him but she twisted out of his grasp and walked off. He felt she'd just given him a very mixed message about her feelings. Would the Sarah he'd connected with last night return to him, or was the bright light of day jerking her back into a reality that he didn't want her to return to?

As he hobbled past the kitchen to the bathroom, he noticed her struggling with a big bag of rubbish.

'Hey, I'll take that out for you if you like, before I shower,' he offered.

She looked at him gratefully. 'Thanks. The bin's still by the front gate. I haven't brought it in yet.'

'No problem,' Ben said. He shot back the double bolts on the front door. It felt strange that Sarah was still so security-conscious when he'd been sleeping on the couch. She must have done it after she left him last night.

He felt some discomfort in his stomach at her vigilance. It wasn't exactly a high crime area here. The worst thing that had happened in the past five years was someone stealing a purse that a swimmer had left on the beach in full view. What made her feel so worried?

As he reached the gate, the bag snagged on a prickly bush and split, pouring rubbish in a messy heap all over the garden path.

Ben swore. 'Wretched bush.' He hated clearing up rubbish. As he gathered up remnants of food and slimy plastic wrappers, his attention was caught by two cream envelopes. They looked vaguely familiar. He picked them up, crumpled and covered in gravy stains. Smoothing them out, he read that unfamiliar name, Amanda Taylor. The envelopes had been opened.

He felt uneasy and looked inside them; they were empty. Things were getting stranger and stranger. Why would Sarah open mail which was addressed to someone else and then throw it away? Surely she would have just returned it to the sender? And if not, why not?

With an inexplicable nervousness, he carefully rummaged around in the bin bag. There was no sign of any letters. What had been in those envelopes? He looked again.

An angry shout interrupted his actions. 'What are you doing, Ben?'

He spun around with an uncomfortable expression on his face. Sarah was standing at the front door looking absolutely furious, her hands on her hips and posture erect.

'Er, the bag split. I was just cleaning it up,' he attempted to explain, his hands still full of scraps of crumpled paper and tin cans. He could hear how guilty he sounded.

'Just leave it,' she snapped. 'And then go home for a shower and breakfast. I'm busy.' She quickly turned and slammed the front door so hard that the bang echoed in his ears.

★　★　★

Sarah turned her CD player up very loudly and stormed around the house, tears pouring down her cheeks. She kicked the kitchen door with force then sank to the floor and hit the cold tiles repeatedly.

'You stupid woman!' she cried, 'Stupid, idiotic, naïve fool!' She had seen him looking through the contents of her bin, not just clearing up some rubbish. Did he think she was born yesterday? Was he spying on her too? She'd had enough of people intruding on her privacy and thinking that they had the right to know every single detail of her life so they could throw it back at her, twisting the truth to suit their needs.

Eventually the adrenaline petered out and she lay curled on the floor feeling deflated and disappointed — disappointed with herself, disappointed with Ben and disappointed that her first glimpse of love for such a long time had ended so quickly and so badly.

Well, it's probably for the best, she

told herself. *Anyway, it was only a bin bag and full of normal stinky rubbish. He probably went home smelling like a tip.* That thought amused her.

As she rose to her feet, she remembered what else she had thrown out.

She cursed loudly and slammed her fists on the wall. Why hadn't she shredded the envelopes as she'd done with the letters? She could only hope that Ben hadn't noticed them. She felt alarmingly close to having her life snatched away from her for a second time.

★   ★   ★

'There you go, young Ben, make sure you look after her well and I'll see you safe and sound back here tomorrow.' Old Joe handed over the keys to his little boat. 'There's that nice cove just up the coast if you want to have a picnic with Amy and Tegan, or otherwise the fishing's good if you're going out with some mates. You've chosen a good day. It's lovely and calm, though I daresay that's not ideal for you surfers.'

Ben hadn't disclosed the real reason why he wanted to borrow Joe's boat. He wanted to keep his love life to himself for the moment. That's if he still had a love life, he mused. He was hoping a nice trip on a boat would be a good way of making things up to Sarah, given how much she loved the sea and felt happiest on the ocean.

He didn't want to think about what would happen if it went wrong and the two of them were trapped on a boat together. She might decide that she didn't want him to live to see another day after all. He knew that he'd been in the wrong, even if he wasn't sure why. He just hoped she'd forgive him.

'Thanks, Joe, see you tomorrow.' He shoved the keys in his pocket and picked up the shopping bags. He had just one hour to make up a picnic hamper and get the boat ready to go.

Nerves jangled through him.

It was two o'clock when he finally knocked on Sarah's front door. There was no reply. That didn't surprise him. She was obviously avoiding him. In the heat of the afternoon, a bead of sweat rolled down his forehead. He wiped it away, gathered himself together and resolutely walked around the side of the house.

Ben spotted Sarah sitting in front of a canvas staring blankly at her work, the patio door slightly ajar to let in some welcome fresh air. He took a deep breath and prised the door open just enough for her to notice his presence.

She looked up at him with a hostile expression. He held up his hands to show he had come in peace. 'Sarah, I am so sorry about earlier,' he said. 'The bag did genuinely tear.' He thought it was better not to disclose what he had chosen to do next. 'I feel so bad that it seems to have affected our friendship.' Ben wasn't sure that it was wise to suggest that they had shared something much more special than companion-ship. 'I really would like the chance to make it up to you.'

There was silence. Ben wasn't sure what else to say.

'Please, Sarah.' His quiet voice held a desperate plea. 'I know that for some reason I've hurt you, but I'd like to have the opportunity to put it right.'

She looked up at him. He noticed the pain in her eyes and was filled with shame. She had trusted him, and he'd been creating fictional mysteries in his head about her integrity.

Slowly she stood up. He stayed paused, waiting for what might come next. Eventually, she walked towards him, still silent. She stopped then held out her arms. He stepped forwards at the gesture, dropped a kiss on her brown curls and took her in his arms, giving her a solid and firm hug. She melted into his embrace.

After a few minutes, she raised her head. 'I'm sorry too,' she said quietly. 'I over-reacted.'

He looked into her sad blue eyes, sensing her raw fear and helplessness. 'That's okay, my darling,' he murmured. 'It'll be okay.'

Tentatively he asked, 'Will you let me make it up to you? I've got a surprise for you, if you'd like . . . '

Sarah gave a shaky little smile. 'A surprise?' she said, 'That sounds exciting.' Ben hesitated and she added, 'Well, don't keep me in suspense.'

'Come with me,' he said, grabbing her keys and cardigan and leading her down to the beach. 'We're in for an afternoon of adventure.'

★ ★ ★

Ben and Sarah lay on the tartan picnic rug on the golden sand. The cove was so secluded that it was exclusively their own for the afternoon. Nobody else had made the long trip along the coast path from the closest village. Sailing there was the quickest and easiest way to access it.

The boat trip had been incredible, Sarah thought. The spray from the bow and the heat of the sun had lifted her spirits. She turned her head and looked at Ben who was blissfully stretched out snoozing in the heat. She realised how badly she had blown things out of proportion earlier.

'It's so beautiful here,' she said. 'Like our own little paradise.' Calmness swept over her. She felt a million miles away from the reality of her life.

'I'm glad I moved here,' she added. 'I just love it. And thank you for this amazing treat. I don't deserve it after this morning. I turned into a hysterical hormonal woman and I wouldn't have blamed you if you hadn't come back.' She fudged the truth slightly.

Ben opened his eyes and looked at her. His tanned face shone in the sunlight. 'I'm glad you moved here, too. And you do deserve to be treated. If Tegan is my princess then you shall be my queen.'

He rolled over and propped himself

up on his elbow, his face just inches from hers. She felt a thrill race through her body as he bent down and kissed her again. She could feel the passion contained behind his gentleness, knowing that he was holding back until she was ready. His thoughtfulness touched her. Ben was a special man, one in a billion, she realised.

It had been a long time since she had trusted anyone. Life was just perfect, she thought. Perfectly perfect. For the first time in many years, she felt relaxed and content.

★　★　★

Ben headed out of Sarah's house later, whistling happily. He couldn't believe that his paranoia had almost wrecked his beautiful relationship with this beautiful woman. He felt somehow complete, as if he had found a missing part of his soul.

He started imagining their future together. He sensed that Sarah would love the wildness and remoteness of the Isles of Scilly. Perhaps he could take her there for a holiday when he next had some time off. He knew Joe's cousin had a holiday cottage there that he could rent.

His thoughts were interrupted by the sight of an official-looking man on his doorstep talking to Amy. She looked distressed and was clutching one of Tegan's teddy bears. He started running in panic.

'Ben, I'm glad you're here,' she cried, 'It's awful!' She was shaking.

'What's wrong, what's happened?' Ben said with urgency, reaching out to touch her shoulder. Images of problems with Tegan or his parents flashed through his mind.

The man turned to him. 'Hello, I'm Dave Lockett, journalist. You must be this lady's brother. Nice to meet you.' He stood poised eagerly with his dictaphone just inches from Ben's chin like a lion waiting to pounce. 'So tell me, what's it like living next door to a murderer?'

'A murderer?' Ben asked in confusion. Both his neighbours either side had been living there for years and were so old that he couldn't see them being capable of murdering as much as a spider. Had something happened in his absence?

'Ben, it's that woman opposite. Look.' Amy shoved a photocopy of a newspaper article at him.

He looked at the headline. *Woman jailed for brutally killing father*, it screamed. Next to it was a photo of a woman with long, blonde curly hair. With a horrible dread in his heart, he examined it more closely. Sarah's face looked blankly back at him. Although she'd had her hair cut and dyed, he'd recognise her anywhere.

Ben read the first paragraph: 'Amanda Taylor sentenced for stabbing ailing dad in the most violent crime of the decade. Judges call for her never to be freed.'

Suddenly bits of the puzzle fell uncomfortably in place: the envelopes, the artwork, Sarah's self-imposed isolation, the security on her house, her lack of family and friends. It all made sense.

'Oh my God,' he said. 'Amy, go indoors at once.'

Pushing the man aside he closed the door firmly behind him, his mind reeling. Slumping to the ground, he trembled in shock and disbelief.

9

Ben stood up and kicked one of Tegan's stray toys, sending it skittering across the floor. 'Are you okay?' Amy's strained face peered at him.

'Does that child have to leave her things lying everywhere, just waiting for someone to fall over?' he shouted. Without waiting for a reply, he stormed up the stairs. Shutting his bedroom door behind him, he sank on to the bed. His eyes stung as he buried his face in the pillow. Nausea rose in his throat. He swallowed hard. The image of Sarah's blue eyes, initially so enticing, now chilled him to the core. He tried to imagine her brutally killing the man she'd claimed to adore. It seemed impossible, Sarah was so kind and sweet, but he'd seen the newspaper clipping for himself.

A bitter taste filled his mouth. Questions buzzed around in his head but nothing made sense. He grabbed viciously at an empty water glass and threw it across the room. It shattered with a satisfying crash.

'Ben.' Amy's voice came through the door. 'Please, Ben, talk to me. I'm worried about you.'

Her voice touched something in him. Deflated, he opened the door. She tilted her head and looked at him. 'Oh Ben, I didn't realise you felt so strongly about her.' She hugged him warmly and suggested they talk in the kitchen, where she could make them some tea.

'Oh, Amy, what am I going to do? Nothing makes sense.' Ben fiddled with the salt pot on the kitchen table and looked to his sister for guidance.

'I don't know,' she said, clutching her mug of tea. 'But on a practical level, she can't be dangerous to the general public otherwise the police would be keeping a close eye on her. And not every murderer goes on to kill a second time. I know you liked her but, well, it's probably best that you found out at this stage . . . I know it doesn't feel like that, though . . . '

Ben looked at his sister. 'Since when did you become so wise?' he said, feeling incredibly fragile. 'Here was me thinking that I was the older one.'

Amy sighed. 'Well, life experiences can make you grow up faster than you want sometimes . . . sadly.'

'But I had suspected that Sarah was the one who'd been in a violent relationship. Then I discover that she killed her father. Her own father! She told me he died from cancer . . . how could I be so wrong?'

Amy thought for a minute. 'Ben, you are the most caring and sensitive man I know. It doesn't surprise me that you looked for the best in her.' She looked straight into his eyes. 'What are you going to do next?'

Ben tried to gather his confused thoughts. There were just too many missing gaps which only one person could fill. 'I'm going to go and talk to her,' he announced.

'Are you sure?' said Amy, her worried eyes studying him intently.

'Yes,' Ben replied, 'I have to do this, then it's over.'

★ ★ ★

Sarah put on her favourite music and waltzed around the cottage. The steam from the kettle misted up the kitchen window. With a youthful impulsiveness, she wrote, 'I love Ben' and smiled to herself.

On impulse, she reached out again and added a kiss at the bottom then surrounded the artwork with a heart. The lettering shone out confidently for a few minutes then started to fade away in the warmth of the summer evening.

Sarah giggled at the fluttering sensation she felt inside her. How long had it been since she had felt so happy and carefree, so loved? She adored everything about Ben; the dimples that lit up his face when he smiled, his gentle touch, his thoughtfulness and great sense

153

of humour. She'd never dared believe that such a man existed, let alone would be interested in her.

The evening sunshine poured into the cottage, lighting up the rooms with its comforting glow. Sarah poured steaming water over a teabag, enjoying the aroma it gave off. She wondered when she would see Ben next. Perhaps she could cook dinner for him tomorrow night. She wondered what his favourite food was.

'Sarah?'

She heard the shout coming from the front door, followed by a determined knocking. He was keen! She put the cup down and danced to the door. As she opened it, he pushed his way into the living room. She tensed. Something felt very wrong. His face was ash-white as he took up a position behind one of her chairs, gripping its back with clenched fists.

'Ben . . . ?' She wasn't sure what to say. 'Is something wrong?' He continued to stand there as if lost for words, the atmosphere explosive. She felt scared. 'Ben, please say something. What's the matter?'

He exhaled strongly. 'I want you to tell me the truth.'

'Of course,' she said, frightened and worried. Had he discovered her secret — but how?

'Are you the Amanda Taylor who killed her father in the most violent crime of the decade?'

She felt faint and sick and tried to open her mouth but the things she needed to say got stuck in her throat. He carried on looking at her. She desperately wanted to turn the clock back, pretend everything was okay. His eyes bore into her, pushing her for answers.

Finally, she spoke. 'I was called Amanda Taylor, yes, but . . . ' Words failed her. It was all so complicated and if she had struggled so much, but failed, to be heard at the time, how could she expect Ben to believe her now? Nobody had ever been on her side.

'I don't see where the 'but' comes

into it,' Ben snapped, not allowing her to finish. 'You told me that you were close to your father and today some journalist turns up on my doorstep and tells me I'm living next door to a murderer. Oh, and not just any murderer, but one who has weaselled her way into my heart using lies and deceit.'

The force of his hatred and hurt hit her and she sobbed. 'Ben, please listen, please. It's not like that. You don't know the whole story.'

'Well, tell me what it is like, then, because I'm not hanging around to be slaughtered like a bull as soon as my usefulness has come to an end!' His caring and reasonable nature was suddenly lost to her. Sarah knew it was a lot for him to take in.

She realised that he wasn't going to listen to her. Old feelings of unfairness and injustice hit her. She should have realised that her past was never going to stop haunting her. Loneliness and sadness filled her soul.

'Ben, I'm sorry. I didn't mean to hurt

you but it's complicated. I think it's better if you leave immediately. I can't talk to you when you're like this.' She was reeling with the force of his feelings and couldn't bear seeing the pain in his eyes any longer.

He angrily pushed the chair away from him. It toppled over and landed on its side, knocking the coffee table as it fell, sending Sarah's cup flying. She instinctively scuttled back to avoid the boiling water which splashed everywhere. Ben walked off, his body stiff. Pausing at the door, he turned.

'I won't be talking to you from now on. Ever. I think it'd be better if you just left. There'll be plenty of people out for your blood anyway when this gets out.' He slammed the door behind him sending shudders through the house. Sarah double bolted it with trembling hands then stood at the window and watched him make his way home.

Ben's words reverberated around her brain. How had a journalist tracked her down? She'd been so careful. The police had been so thorough, too, apart from the glitch which meant she'd had a few official letters in her old name. But who would have traced that?

If one journalist had been tipped off, then it wouldn't be long before others joined in the witch hunt and the terror would start all over again. The unfairness of it choked her and a sense of defeat flooded through her body. She wished that she'd never moved here.

Ben was right, she couldn't stay here any longer. She felt empty and dead; she didn't know if she wanted to live anywhere any more. The events of the last two years weighed her down like a permanent ball and chain. She had no energy to keep moving forward any more.

Sarah shivered and pulled her cardigan tightly around her. As she did so, her fingers touched a lump in her pocket. Dipping her hand in, she drew out a small bunch of keys.

Looking at them, she realised they were the keys for the boat that Ben had borrowed. He'd asked her to hold them whilst he was securing the craft and then had forgotten to ask for them back. It seemed so long ago now, she thought wistfully. Fingering them, an idea came into her head. She knew what she had to do. Grabbing her thick fleece top, Sarah crept out the back door under the cover of dusk.

★　★　★

Amy saw Ben run across the road and up the drive, throwing himself through the door. They looked at each other.

'Don't ask,' he said, 'But it's finished. I told her to leave the village too. Hopefully she'll do a runner quite quickly, especially now she knows the press are after her.'

'Oh, Ben.' Amy gazed at him with compassion in her eyes, 'I'm sorry. Is there anything I can do?'

'No, thank you anyway.' He looked at her properly this time. Why was she standing in such an odd way with her hand behind her? He caught a glimpse of white.

'What's that?' He pointed behind her. She flushed and avoided his gaze.

'Oh, nothing . . . '

'Amy?' His tone was stern. 'Show me.'

Reluctantly she brought a stack of paper into view. 'Well, you know I'm not that good on the internet but I was just trying to find out a bit more.' She looked embarrassed.

'Can I see?'

Amy flinched. 'It's not good. Are you sure you want to?'

Ben faltered for a minute. Was he sure? He wasn't certain about many of his choices any more. All he was sure of was that it couldn't get any worse and this way at least he'd know the harsh details without having to talk to Sarah. She would probably just fob him off with more excuses anyway. It might help to give him closure on the relationship.

'Yes, I'm sure. Please?'

Amy reluctantly handed the paper over to him and disappeared.

Ben felt ill. Hours of reading and re-reading damning newspaper reports, blog opinions and viewing graphic images had been sickening. He was glad he'd looked at it but part of him wished he was still living in blissful ignorance. Usually he avoided news stories like the plague, content to live in his little bubble of surfing, family and work. National events didn't interest him very much but he wondered how he could have missed this one.

He clearly wasn't the only person who was angry with Sarah. An internet hate campaign was raging against her, there were calls for the death sentence to be reintroduced to Britain and petitions for Sarah to be locked up forever. However much he tried, he couldn't think of her as Amanda.

Amy put her head around his bedroom door.

'Hey, you okay?' She handed him a mug of hot chocolate with his favourite squirt of whippy cream and chocolate sprinkles. Just like he'd had as a child, he thought.

'Yes, you were right. It's awful but I'm glad you gave it to me. I had to know.' He shook his head. 'I think I need to sleep, though.' He glanced at the clock. 'It's gone midnight.'

As Amy left, he cradled the mug in his hands, enjoying its warmth and sweetness. He hoped things might feel better in the morning.

But sleep refused to knock him into a state of unconsciousness. He tossed and turned, his brain trying to make sense of everything he'd read, everything he knew about Sarah. At four o'clock, he gave up lying there, his initial anger having died down and replaced by a desire to get the facts straight in his head. Something was niggling him.

He poured over the internet print-outs for the billionth time. None of them mentioned why Sarah had been released from jail or what the 'technicality' was that had let her out. He was also baffled by how happy she was when she talked about her father and her tears when she admitted he was dead.

Were those the signs of a killer? They had come across as tears of sadness rather than tears of guilt and remorse. And what about the scar on her leg, or was that just a childhood accident?

Ben remembered the softness of her body and the light touch of her hands on his skin. Lots of things didn't fit but he wondered if his desperation to retain his loving image of Sarah was blinding him to the stark facts.

There must be more to this, he thought, *there just has to be*. He switched on his laptop and started his own internet search.

★   ★   ★

Ben rubbed his gritty, sore eyes and yawned. He hadn't filled many gaps in his knowledge. If anything, he had more questions to answer. Reports said that Sarah had been released after new evidence came to light which questioned the reliability of the police forensics but details they gave were vague. They had been forced to free her but opinion was that it was just a matter of time before they were able to re-convict her.

Sarah was under police protection because of the strength of public feeling. That didn't surprise him, but it didn't make him feel any better either. He realised that he'd been hoping to find some happy ending, something that restored his faith in her. There was none.

Ben lay back on his bed. He needed to surf to restore his equilibrium, but it was too early yet, the tide wasn't right. He put his hand out, fumbled to switch on the radio hoping to catch the weather and surf report.

He dozed on the bed, lulled by the soothing voices of the morning breakfast show presenters talking about the traffic, the state of the economy and farming in Cornwall. He felt himself relax as sleep finally washed over him and he dozed blissfully for a while.

The beeps that signalled the start of

the morning news bulletin dragged him back to consciousness. He stretched, enjoying his sleepy limbo.

'And the main news story this morning,' the presenter announced in her serious tones, 'A shocking new development in the Manchester murder case following the recent controversial release of Amanda Taylor.'

Ben sat bolt upright and turned up the volume as the presenter continued. 'Police last night formally arrested Mrs Taylor's ex-husband, Stuart Taylor, on suspicion of murder and attempting to pervert the course of justice. New evidence suggests that Mr Taylor, who had serious gambling debts, framed his wife for the murder of her father, Timothy Harding, after killing him in an attempt to claim his inheritance. No further details have been given but top legal experts are calling for a full investigation into this tragic miscarriage of justice. A full police statement is expected later.'

The presenter moved on to the next story. Ben froze with shock, replaying the news over and over in his head.

His bedroom door flew open. Amy stood there in her dressing gown, hair unkempt and face etched with worry. 'You heard the news?' she asked, watching him as he fiddled with his radio. 'Ben, I think you should look out of the window. Didn't you hear the noise?'

He leapt out of bed and flung back the curtains. Police cars blocked the narrow road, which was already crowded with people, television crews and photographers with long-lens cameras. Satellite dishes sprouted like mushrooms on several vans, all ready and waiting to beam the latest news pictures worldwide.

Ben could see the police officers trying to hold the masses back as they all pushed to get a glimpse of Sarah's cottage in the hope of seeing her.

He cursed loudly, shoving his legs into his jeans and pulling his T-shirt over his head.

'What are you doing?' Amy asked in alarm.

'I'm going out there. I have to be

with her, she'll be so scared. God, I've been such an idiot! She has to forgive me, she has to. You just stay indoors and keep everything locked.'

He grabbed his trainers and muscled his way out into the street. People were everywhere; on his driveway, trampling over the flowerbeds and trying to stand on his car bonnet for a better view. He was horrified at their morbid greediness as they tried to grab all the gory details of Sarah's ordeal, all wanting the first pictures of her and the first interviews. It disgusted him.

'Are you and your family all right, sir?' A policeman, noticing that Ben had come out of the house, came to check on him.

'Yes, but please tell me. Is Sarah okay?'

'I can't give out personal details, sir.'

Ben desperately put his hand on the man's shoulder and guided him to one side away from the crowds. 'Please, at least tell me that. My name is Ben Trelawny and Sarah — um, Amanda

— is my girlfriend. I have to know. It looks like a bloodbath waiting to happen out here.'

The policeman shook his head as if processing the rules and regulations, then fixed Ben with a confidential gaze. He spoke in a low voice so nobody else could hear him. 'Well, this is strictly private information, but I'm afraid we don't know where the lady is. We've been here since dawn but the cottage is empty and there's no sign of anyone. All her things are still there, though, so it's unlikely that she'll have left the area.'

Ben felt his throat go dry and he ran back indoors.

'Amy!' he cried, then spotting his sister said, 'She's gone missing. I have to look for her. Where's my rescue rucksack?' He was referring to the bag that he took with him when holiday makers lost their children and sparked hunts along the coastline.

'It's in the cupboard under the stairs. I've just boiled the kettle so I'll make a flask. You grab some food.'

As they worked quickly, the phone rang. Amy picked it up. 'No, he's busy at the moment,' she said, 'Yes, I'll tell him . . . can it wait until tomorrow, though? Great . . . thanks.'

She came back to him and seeing his strained face said, 'Don't worry, that was just Joe asking for his boat keys back. He said there's no hurry.'

Ben paused for a second then his brow creased into a frown. 'No!' he shouted, slapping his forehead with the palm of his hand in his frustration. Now he remembered where he had last seen the keys.

10

Ben scrambled up the cliff path, stumbling on its unevenness. The boat was missing from its mooring place just as he'd feared. He frantically scanned the ocean several times, praying to see the little yellow vessel bobbing up and down.

The sea spread out in front of him, calm and brilliant blue, a stark contrast to the turmoil Ben that felt inside. Guilt ate at him. Sarah had tried to explain everything and he had been too blinded by his own emotions to hear her out. Now, she had taken the boat and disappeared, probably late last night after the argument. There wasn't much diesel left in it either; he'd been meaning to refill it this morning before he returned it.

What if something had happened to her? Or what if his rejection had led to her do something stupid? He wouldn't blame her. He was the only person in the world that she was starting to trust and he'd let her down.

Ben wondered if he should ring the coastguard but thought the publicity of a full-scale search was exactly what Sarah didn't need at the moment. If she didn't return, it would be different. He shivered — he didn't want to think that far ahead, but he wasn't sure what other reason anyone would have for taking out a small sailing vessel in the dark. It had rained last night too. It wasn't looking good but at least she could handle the boat, probably better than him. Where would she have gone? She didn't even know the area.

It was then he remembered the small cove a mile down the bay where they'd shared their picnic. It was his last hope. Strapping his rucksack firmly on to his back, he raced along the coast path.

The cove lay peaceful in the morning sun. Ben scaled the steep steps down the cliff. The yellow boat was beached on the sand. His heart leapt in relief and his eyes searched the beach. It was bare.

★ ★ ★

The coldness gnawed at Sarah's bones as she drifted in and out of consciousness. She tried to lift her head off the ground but it felt incredibly heavy and wouldn't move. Her body was too tired, she had no will to go on.

'Sarah!' She was vaguely aware of her name being called, first distantly then getting closer.

'Dad?' she murmured faintly, barely able to speak. 'Dad, is that you?'

It was all right now; it was all over. She was at peace, and her dad had come to get her, just as she'd begged him to as she'd staggered, soaking wet into the cave last night.

She heard footsteps and saw a light shining into her eyes. *Is this it?* she thought and mentally willed herself to slip down the tunnel quickly and return to the loving care of her father.

'Sarah, thank God,' a male voice said as comforting hands slid under her body and scooped her off the hard, gritty sand. Warmth enveloped her. She groaned and lapsed back into sleepiness. It was okay . . . everything would be okay now . . .

★ ★ ★

Ben staggered back out into the brightness of the sun with Sarah hanging limply in his arms. Dropping his torch, he gently laid her in the soft sand above the high tide line.

'Sarah, can you hear me?' he asked urgently, shaking her shoulder and rummaging around in his rucksack. He felt the dampness of her fleece and carefully peeled it off her, replacing it with a warm wool jumper and enfolding her in his foil hypothermia blanket.

She groaned again and said groggily, 'Dad?'

He wasn't sure whether he should

shatter her illusion yet. She looked pale and fragile, her skin clammy to the touch. It frightened him.

'It's all right, Sarah, you're really cold but you should start to feel better soon.' He reached under the blanket and found her hand. 'Grasp my hand if you can hear me.' A weak squeeze lightly touched his skin. He sighed with relief. 'I need you to keep talking to me, Sarah. Please stay with me.'

Her head moved slightly and her lips twitched but no sound came out.

'Hey, you're doing fine,' he reassured her, sounding more confident than he felt. 'Just stay with me. It's really important.' He had so much that he wanted to say but it would have to wait. 'You scared me, you know.' He put his hand on her forehead and tenderly stroked it.

He tried to make a joke of the situation. 'I thought you might have tried to sail across the Atlantic to America in Joe's tiny boat. That's next week's trip when we've got more supplies.'

She let out a small moan.

'Sarah, I need you to open your eyes, my love. I've got some hot coffee and a chocolate bar in my bag.' He laughed. A little smile formed on her face and brought him relief. She slowly opened her eyes, squinting in the brightness. He moved around to shade her so that she could see him.

'Ben?' she asked in confusion.

'Yes, it's me. It's so good to have you back. I've never been so happy to see you. Oh, Sarah, I'm so sorry about everything. I know I was wrong. There's something I've got to tell you that will change everything for the better.' He wasn't sure if this was the right time but he was desperate.

'Tell me.' She looked more alert. 'No more secrets.'

He started to tell her what had happened.

* * *

Sarah sat huddled under her blanket sipping the coffee and nibbling at the

175

chocolate. Her head spun at the news; it was almost too much to take in. After all this time, after everything she had been put through. She'd pleaded with everyone to believe her and they hadn't. Instead, they had put her through intense suffering and accused her of killing her darling father, the man she adored. There was no worse insult.

But the truth was out now. She felt like she'd been given a new chance but she was also angry at being labelled a criminal. The pain ran deep. Dread filled her as she thought about being harassed by the media again as they conveniently forgot how they condemned her before and now eagerly sought to portray her as the victim.

Hypocrites, she thought with resentment. She didn't want either identity.

She looked at Ben. He was checking that the boat was moored properly now that the tide was starting to come in. She couldn't believe he'd come after her, after everything that had happened, and she wondered whether his motives were as true as he said — perhaps it was just guilt that had driven him to look for her. Guilt over his hasty assumptions and angry outburst.

Sadness swept over her. She closed her eyes for a while, drifting away from reality and enjoying the sensation of the sun heating her bones. He eventually returned to where she sat.

'How are you feeling?' he asked. The kindness in his voice moved her.

'Much warmer, thanks,' she said. 'I'll live to see another day.' They grinned at their shared joke.

He dropped on to his knees next to her. 'Sarah, I am really sorry about how I reacted last night. I should have given you a chance to explain.'

'Ben, you really scared me. I thought I could trust you. How can you expect me to forget all that?' Her voice was filled with hurt.

'I can't,' he said honestly. 'I was just so shocked, felt so betrayed, and I knew you were hiding something. But this? I mean, it was devastating to hear that sort of news. How would you have felt if you'd been me?' His voice trailed off.

They sat in silence for a moment, looking out to sea, then she turned to him. 'Ben, you're right. I can't imagine what it must have felt like to you. I think I'd have been very angry too.'

'But it was unfair of me not to listen to you,' he interrupted. 'I'm guessing that I probably just repeated an old and familiar theme in your life. I can't imagine what you've had to endure. It must have been a living nightmare.'

She was touched by his sensitivity.

'As you just said, no more secrets. Sarah, so I would feel very privileged if you still felt able to tell me your story. As much as you feel able to. I want to understand, to support you, my darling.'

She looked at his broad hand which was caressing her knee and stared straight into his face, noticing the firmness of his jaw and slightly weathered skin. His eyes were full of compassion and love.

'Okay, but it's not a pretty story,' she warned him.

'I sort of know bits of it . . . the media, you know . . . ' He flushed slightly. 'But I'm guessing that's quite a sensationalist angle.'

'Yes, I think you should have the rest of this chocolate and I'll fill you in.' She handed it to him and began to tell her story.

'I was always very close to my father, as you know. Shortly after my mother died, when I was twenty-five, I met Stuart. I was young and impressionable, and also grieving and desperate for love andsecurity. He was a successful businessman and was so much fun. Everyone wanted to be his girlfriend but he chose me; I felt so special and fell hopelessly in love with him and we married within six months.

'Dad was devastated — he quickly saw through Stuart's charm — but I wouldn't listen to him. Shortly after our marriage, Dad was diagnosed with cancer, a very slow-growing one but with quite a good prognosis. I worried about him living alone so persuaded

Stuart to convert our extension into an annexe for him. Dad jokingly called it a 'Grandad flat', although we never gave him any grandchildren . . . thank God.'

Sarah shivered and swallowed hard before continuing. 'For the next year, Dad was in and out of hospital. The doctors thought he would go into remission but nothing was guaranteed. In the meantime, I discovered that Stuart was drinking and gambling heavily. On a good night, he'd come home and expect me to continue partying with him into the early hours. On a bad night, he'd come home and . . . ' she shuddered at the memory, 'He'd hit me . . . or worse . . . '

She fell silent. Ben held her hand firmly in his. 'Oh, sweetheart,' he said, and waited for her to go on.

'Dad kept begging me to leave but I felt trapped. Stuart was a very powerful husband; he took control of everything and we had no money. He wouldn't let me go to work and made me feel that I was totally useless. One night he smashed up all my art stuff and told me

180

I was just an amateur playing with paints. Over time, he gradually eroded my confidence and I became stuck at home, trying to ward off the debt collectors and hide the alcohol. It was awful.' Tears finally came into her eyes.

'After one particularly bad beating, Dad told me that he'd had enough and that he'd planned for us to leave together for Canada. We have cousins there. He'd booked the flights for a week's time, long enough for us to sort out his medical care, tie up loose ends and cover our tracks.

'Then, one morning, when I'd taken Dad to the hospital for his last follow-up appointment, Stuart broke into the annex, presumably to look for money, and found Dad's packed bag with our tickets and passports. He also had a copy of his will in there. It showed that he would leave a considerable amount of money to me when he died.' Her body tensed.

'When we got home, Stuart confronted us about our plans to leave and

Dad collapsed. I put him to bed and pleaded with Stuart to leave him alone in return for me staying. When Dad was stable, I left him so I could cook dinner. When I got back, he was dead.'

She paused then continued in a wobbly voice, 'Stuart had suffocated him with a pillow. I screamed and screamed, shaking Dad in the hope that I could bring him back but knowing it was too late. Stuart said he had my money and it was what we deserved. I snapped and told him that Dad had written a clause into his will that meant my husband had no claim on my inheritance. That tipped him over the edge and he violently attacked poor Dad's body with a carving knife . . . ' Her words came out in gasps and sobs. 'I tried to stop him . . . but when I got in the way and he slashed me . . . '

Ben instinctively reached out and took her in his arms, holding her tightly to him. 'The scar on your leg?' he asked. She looked confused. 'Tegan told me,' he added.

'Yes, but he said I did it to myself.' She grimaced. 'Dad . . . my poor Dad . . . It was my fault. I should have listened to him earlier.'

'Hush,' Ben soothed. 'It wasn't your fault, it could never be your fault. Stuart was an evil man.'

She continued as if he hadn't spoken, in a desperate rush to get the next words out. 'And then Stuart twisted all the evidence to make it look like I'd done it and nobody believed me when I said that was a lie. Everyone turned against me. Even my own solicitor doubted me. Stuart had altered many of his debts so that they were in my name, bribing people to lie about it for him. Whatever I said, nobody believed me.' She clung on to Ben, the dampness of her tears seeping into his T-shirt.

'I'm sorry,' Ben said. 'Hush, sweetheart, hush.' He rocked her like a baby. 'You're safe with me. I'll never let anyone else hurt you. You're far too precious to me. Why do you think I came to find you? I was so worried that you had drowned. I had visions of finding your body washed up on the coastline. I want you in my life, not anywhere else.'

Sarah looked straight into his eyes through a veil of tears. 'How do I know that?' she said bitterly. 'How can I trust you?' She loosened her grasp and moved away from him a little. 'No, I have to leave here and start afresh, somewhere else. Somewhere new, where nobody knows me. I can leave the country now my innocence has been proved . . . just disappear overseas.'

Ben's expression changed and he looked like a lost little boy.

'Sarah, please . . . I need you. I made a massive mistake but I can see how wrong I was. Please stay. As long as we're together, we can deal with anything. Everyone will leave you alone soon, you'll see . . . the focus will turn on to Stuart and we can just get on with our lives and be happy. People will slowly forget who you are and the locals around here are fiercely protective of their own. You're one of us now.'

She avoided his gaze, not wanting to see the emotion in his face.

'And, Sarah, if you run away, you'll be running forever. Is that what you really want?'

Her instincts told her that getting out of the situation was the safest move but she also craved his closeness. Being held in his arms and listening to his heart beating next to hers gave her a sense of security that she'd forgotten had existed. Now she'd been reeled in by that, could she live without it?

'I'm not Stuart,' Ben added. 'I'm just a surfer dude who's happy with his life, lives with his sister and loves hanging out on the beach. I spend my life with a toddler dangling upside down in my hands thinking I'm a mobile playground and I have a reputation for smuggling food out of the kitchen when Amy's not looking. What you see is what you get!' He hoped that his light-hearted attempt at persuading Sarah to see his integrity would work.

She sat there turning things over and

over in her head. Who knew what would be for the best?

They sat there for a while, the stillness only broken by the sea lapping at the shore and the odd seagull crying overhead. Sarah felt unsure, her heart telling her one thing, her head arguing another.

'There's also something I need you to see,' Ben added mysteriously.

Sarah's attention was recaptured. 'What's that?' she asked curiously.

He pulled her to her feet, her blanket dropping to the ground.

'Look.' He pointed to the beach behind her.

Obediently, she shuffled around, still feeling a bit shaky on her legs, his hands steadying her. What she saw brought tears to her eyes, but tears of joy this time. A big heart was drawn in the sand. The biggest heart she'd ever seen. She peered at the words written in it.

'Sarah D, will you marry me?'

A huge smile spread over Sarah's face. All her doubts evaporated.

He was right, if she started running away again, then she would never stop — and perhaps she didn't need to run any more. She spun around to face him, speechless.

He looked worried at her silence. 'I mean, I'm not trying to rush things. We don't have to hurry, we could have the longest engagement on earth,' he said hastily, worried that he'd rushed things too quickly. 'Er, I need to go and look at the boat.'

He started walking off down the beach, but she grabbed his arm, drawing him back, tugging him close.

'Ben — oh, Ben.' She reached up and tangled her fingers through his hair, pulling him close. His lips hovered just inches from hers and she could smell his salt-scented masculinity. Her insides quivered.

Without stopping to give an answer, she gently pressed her lips to his, feeling the roughness of his stubble, and then kissed him with a passion that set every nerve on fire. He responded with joy.

Finally, Sarah broke off and stepped back, running her hands down over his broad shoulders and cupping his hands in hers.

'Just make sure you buy me another chocolate éclair,' she laughed, 'The last one met with a messy ending.'

Ben grinned. 'I'm afraid I also owe you a saffron cake too.' Sarah looked puzzled. 'Um . . . long story, but it doesn't matter. Nothing matters any more. Sarah, I love you so much.' He bent down to kiss her again.

'Me too,' she murmured contentedly, her face glowing with love for him. 'Let's stay here forever.'

THE END

We do hope that you have enjoyed reading this large print book.

Did you know that all of our titles are available for purchase?

We publish a wide range of high quality large print books including:
Romances, Mysteries, Classics
General Fiction
Non Fiction and Westerns

Special interest titles available in large print are:
The Little Oxford Dictionary
Music Book, Song Book
Hymn Book, Service Book

Also available from us courtesy of Oxford University Press:
Young Readers' Dictionary
(large print edition)
Young Readers' Thesaurus
(large print edition)

For further information or a free brochure, please contact us at:
Ulverscroft Large Print Books Ltd.,
The Green, Bradgate Road, Anstey,
Leicester, LE7 7FU, England.
Tel: (00 44) **0116 236 4325**
Fax: (00 44) **0116 234 0205**

Other titles in the
Linford Romance Library:

BOHEMIAN RHAPSODY

Serenity Woods

Elfie Summers is an archaeologist with a pet hate of private collectors. Cue Gabriel Carter, a self-made millionaire. He invites Elfie to accompany him to Prague to verify the authenticity of an Anglo-Saxon buckle, said to grant true love to whoever touches it. And whilst Gabriel's sole motive is to settle an old score, Elfie just wants to return to her quiet, scholarly life — but the city and the buckle have other ideas . . .

LOVE AND CHANCE

Susan Sarapuk

When schoolteacher Megan bumps into a gorgeous Frenchman in the Hall of Mirrors at Versailles, she thinks she will never see him again. Until the Headteacher asks her to visit Lulu Santerre, a pupil who is threatening not to return to school. Megan discovers that Lulu's brother Raphael is the man she met at Versailles . . . When Lulu goes missing Raphael and Megan are thrown together and both of them have to make decisions about their future.

WISH YOU WERE HERE?

Sheila Holroyd

Cara was hoping to spend Christmas in England with her boyfriend, but her mother sweeps her off to a holiday home in Spain. However, they are forced to stay in a hotel, wondering if they can afford the bill. There, she becomes attracted to Nick, despite his being ten years her junior. But, unexpectedly, her boyfriend, Geoff, and Nick's girlfriend, Lily, appear at the hotel. Then both Nick's and Cara's fathers add to the complicated network of relationships . . .

CLOSER!

Julia Douglas

Jess Watkins realises that she's a dreamer with no ambitions when her friend Becky gets married. However, she manages to land herself a job as secretary at the Brachan Window Company. Her boss, Jared King, makes a big impression on her — and not just professionally. But she finds that Jared is married to Suzanne. Then, her career begins to blossom, although the office seems in danger of closing. Working in a double-dealing world, can Jess ever find true love?

FINALLY A FAMILY

Moyra Tarling

He was her first and only love. Claire MacInnes knew she'd encounter him again someday; even imagining what she'd say — so he wouldn't guess her secret. But now, that someday had come, Claire wasn't ready to face Daniel Hunter, or the feelings rushing back. How could she lie to the man she'd never forgotten — or to the daughter she'd struggled to raise alone? The daughter Daniel didn't know existed. Yet Claire wasn't ready to tell the truth yet, either . . .